THE CHRISTMAS BARGAIN

Joan Bird

ALSO BY JOAN BIRD

Tumbleweed Heights
Sam's Gift
Wishes and Miracles
The Week of Living Dangerously
Oscar in Rescued
An Unexpected Rescue in Heart Beat

www.BOROUGHSPUBLISHINGGROUP.com

THE CHRISTMAS BARGAIN
Copyright © 2020 Joan Bird

ISBN 978-1-953810-23-6

To my brother, Edward "Ned" Hosken, 02/10/49 to 05/22/19

Ned, I doubt you'd drop whatever you're doing up there, certainly not to see yourself in the form of a bit-part, a toddler no less, and in a romance novel of all places. But, anything's possible in heaven, so maybe you'll be floating in a restored wooden boat that doesn't leak. Like I said, anything's possible in heaven. Once you get past the first fifteen pages before pronouncing in your no BS way, "Well, this is a load of..."

Miss you, bro. JB

ACKNOWLEDGMENTS

It's funny how writers often appear negligent in communicating the simplest of feelings in the real world yet they manage – hopefully with some eloquence – to infuse their stories with all the emotion necessary for love and a happily ever after. This acknowledgement then, recognizes three parts of the process. No matter what talent a writer might think they possess, it's a gift to be provided a skilled editor and a dedicated publisher. My thanks to Susan. She lent gentle direction (clubs are so uncivilized), non-toxic suggestions, and invaluable assistance for the finished product. A shout out of continued thanks to Boroughs Publishing Group for dedication to story, all things romance, and opportunities for submissions without torture.

Finally, kudos to my sister, Kate Moore, who directed my horrid first efforts at this craft with boatloads of skill and even greater kindness. She is an accomplished and award-winning writer of romantic fiction, with a way of softening even the stodgiest of characters into HEA. As to characters, Kate in *The Christmas Bargain,* is complete fiction. I intended no resemblance to my real-life sibling but used the namesake Kate because it intones strength. Also, because it allowed me these few lines to thank her for being a protagonist of sorts to our extended family of swashbucklers, scholars, and book-addicts. Like all heroines,

And, because, as I hope one day to do, Kate rocks romance.

THE CHRISTMAS BARGAIN

Chapter 1

December 10, 2019

Why didn't I take a cab? God knew Kate hated the subway. There were too many people, at least at 8 a.m. After the last stop, the car she was in had partially emptied, and she'd hoped to grab a seat, but then a new mob of people boarded. Kate now found herself holding on to an overhead strap. The bigger worry was that someone else would squeeze in before the doors closed. Result? Sharing with a stranger.

"Sorry about this, ma'am." The man had a drawl of some kind and towered over Kate by at least six inches, which meant he logged in at about six feet two. He had broad shoulders, enough so she couldn't see around him, and he smelled delicious.

"Whatever." She didn't care one whit about being in a charitable spirit even if the mandatory be-nice season was pretty much crashing down on all of NYC. Kate wondered if anybody else crowded into the car felt the same way.

"That's kind of a bah humbug response, ma'am."

"Please refrain from speaking to me. If you find that impossible, cease and desist from calling me ma'am." There was nothing she could do about the fact that he grabbed the metal "strap" above her right hand. Big whoop. She didn't have to be pleasant about it. The train lurched, slamming the uninvited co-tenant into Kate's chest. At least she was in a thick coat, except the wool was also making her sweat.

"Miss or Mrs.?"

Kate didn't answer. Instead she tried to distance herself from the nosy drawler by at least an inch or two. At that moment, a large woman on the other side of the car twisted around, and a big bag of something slammed into Kate's left hip. "Ow."

"Want I should shoot that package, ma'am?"

His gentle teasing tone gave Kate the courage to dare a look up. By all things holy, the stranger pressing into her was astonishingly gorgeous. Ocean blue eyes with sparks around the irises revealed his amusement at their current predicament. "Yes, please."

"Left my six-shooter back at the ranch, but I could try tackling the thing." Kate was unable to shift her gaze away from his face, as if some magnetic field had them suspended, forcing her to study the laugh lines on either side of his oh-too-sexy eyes. A trace of dark stubble around his chin and upper lip presented an image worthy of the page of a romance novel, fitting of her profession. After all, reading volumes of the stuff was her stock in trade.

The stranger's right hand reached over Kate's shoulder, tapping on the woman's arm holding the attack-parcel. "Pardon me, ma'am. Could we re-situate a little? I'm afraid that bag of yours is prodding my gal."

Kate muttered under her breath, "I am so *not* your gal."

"Oh my. I am sorry, dear," the other woman exclaimed. "Did I hurt you? It's difficult shopping for grandchildren and getting on the subway. Frankly, I'm exhausted. I've come from one of those starts-at-four-a.m. sales, and I'm too old for that kind of thing anymore. Awful, simply awful, but I did manage to pick up everything needed for my three grandchildren. See?" The shop-a-lot Grandma lifted the big reusable bag in the air, and it slammed into Kate's hip again. "Oh my, oh dear, oh…"

"It's okay, ma'am." Now Kate sounded like the subway cowboy. "We're all so packed in here. A little jostling is not surprising. Can I help you with that?" She motioned with her chin to the errant package.

"No, I'm all right, but thank you. My stop is another two minutes. I'll turn this way a little."

Without asking, subway guy unhinged Kate's hand from their strap and shifted her to his left, after which he stepped in between the two women. Kate's brain was self-entertaining by imagining the woman as a fairytale witch who lured small children to her home for fattening. She'd no clue as to why, except that the cowboy was unsettling. She envisioned a pathway scattered with toys, but then shook off the thoughts. The older woman was simply a nice lady who cared for her grandkids. The subway cowboy—maybe not so much.

At least his attention remained averted. For now, anyway. He seemed occupied with making the package grandmother comfortable for the short ride to her stop. He even had her bag in his right hand. Oddly, a pang of disappointment at having lost his attention flooded Kate's limbs. It was as if her hands had fallen asleep, and there was a buzzing between her ears.

The train squealed to a stop, and when the doors opened, her cowboy leaned in, whispering in her ear, "Hold my spot, little lady," followed by a low chuckle that vibrated in her ear and down to her toes. Turning away, he hefted the cumbersome package and helped the grandmother of three out to the platform. Some rude folks simultaneously forced their way in, despite still-departing passengers. It bugged Kate, but she couldn't control everything.

Subway cowboy got the woman beyond the yellow line, where, with a surprise ending, a younger man with green hair, dressed all in black and sporting a chain through his belt loops, offered to help the lady along from there.

Disappointment returned. But why? Seriously, after the "little lady" bit? She would *so* not hold his spot. *Jerk.*

All Kate had wanted to do this morning was get to her desk to work on some editing, hoping there would be a new book good enough to suck her in so the hours would whiz by. She had the power to destroy a tender-hearted writer's dreams with any number of singular words.

1. No. 2. Rejected. 3. Not Submitted within Publisher Guidelines.

Well, that wasn't one word, but it had the same result. Kate would often send a personal note, however short, to the rejectee. Sometimes she offered encouragement. Other times, she'd jot a few in-margin ideas for changes that might result in a successful resubmission.

Of late, her supervising editor, Matthew Andrews, had informed her this method of operation needed to cease. There was to be no mollycoddling—his archaic word. If she had any courage at all she'd have mentioned that usage to the insufferable and arrogant Mr. Andrews. Kate visualized him with a blah-blah-blah cartoon bubble over his head.

Then, unbidden—another archaic word, but she liked it—she visualized a handsome, maybe-moving-to-New-York cowboy. Of course he might be only a tourist, rendering any fantasies useless. Besides, Kate knew herself well. She wasn't afraid of men. Her fear lay in the fact that relationships involved the parties winding up in bed. Still, something about the cowboy drawl had rattled her, and she closed her eyes against an inexplicable feeling of loss.

***

Caleb jumped back onto the train while the doors were closing. As it happened, passengers jostling and grabbing onto empty seats, straps, and poles gave him a chance to step closer to the lanky redhead with green eyes. The woman was downright skinny, but she had a strong chin and freckles. These mapped her face like thousands of islands in the South Pacific. He liked freckles. On the other hand, the tenacity that sparked in her eyes didn't cause him concern. It was the obvious uncertainty she had in herself. She'd also proven to be a snappy comeback girl, and that intrigued the hell out of Cal.

How did a guy pick up a girl on a subway in New York City? He had no problem with the women at home, but most gals he met in Texas were interested in ranching. Hell, they could pitch hay, brand a calf, and chop wood. A beer and one dance of country two-step equaled a date in his part of the world.

Notwithstanding a small personal fortune, many women who'd expressed an interest were in it for the land, not stocks and bonds. He *should* like a girl who could break a wild pony and build a campfire, but one such gal had broken his heart. He'd managed to sew the bits and pieces back together enough that he'd righted his life. In the months after his ex-wife left, he'd become his own self-help book. In truth, the breakup was his fault mostly due to the deep scars of his childhood.

He had no intention of spending years on a psychiatrist's couch reliving his past, his severed childhood, or his losses. It was all crap, and nobody was going to force him into figuring it out. He shook his head to clear the dust, pissed off that he'd lost sight of the gal he'd been sharing a strap with. Then a heavyset man stepped away, and there she was—the gal. He took a moment to study her worried look, then closed the gap between them.

"Howdy, ma'am. Did ya miss me?"

She didn't miss a beat. "I did, terribly. Total loss. Thought I might succumb from a fractured heart right here on the spot. Get carried away by some impartial EMTs—well, they would care. Those first responders are drawn that way, you know. But I'd still be an unknown, destined for a pauper's grave and two mandatory death notice lines in the *Times*. Sigh."

He stepped closer, regaining the overhead strap with his left hand, and stared at the top of his new buddy's head. "You're hilarious. I thought being funny in elevators and on subways was verboten. And you're not unknown, ma'am. Not if you tell me your name."

"So not happening." The gal whose space he invaded shuttered her eyes and muttered, "You smell good." She continued to avoid his gaze with an apparent study of his chin.

The contradiction between refusing to identify herself and tossing out a compliment forced a low chuckle. "Nice to meet you. You smell nice too, but not perfume-y, more like you got caught in a rainstorm in a wool coat."

"I did." She looked up then, and he sensed a forced bravery in the act.

"Sure you did. It was starting to drizzle a little out there. That's a good smell, wet wool." The woman's expression suggested he'd pushed too far. Cal half expected her to quit bantering, whip out a cell phone and call the white coats as soon as she stepped off the train. "Right up there with the smell of horses and saddle leather, and throw in a little cow dung. Nothing like it, ma'am." He smiled, but she was still trying to pretend disinterest. "You know, it's cold in New York this time of year."

"Duh."

"I love an articulate woman who smells like wet wool, especially one who has certain coltish qualities." Cal noticed her eyes widen at the comment. He'd also noted her long legs. She prickled and raised a hand as if to push him away.

"Uh-uh, that's not neighborly." He held a hand up himself as if warding her off, still grinning. He wasn't a gambling man, but he was quite sure the woman was as angry as a bee caught under a saddle blanket. Given the circumstances, he moved back an inch. Given the subway crowd, it was about all the leeway he had unless he jumped off the train.

***

Kate had been momentarily lost in the smell of soap, and maybe aftershave, though it wasn't cloying like some of the suits she'd met in the last few years. It wasn't sticky enough in terms of smell, more like a no-frills bar of supermarket fare. Something with oatmeal and maybe lemon? She had tried ignoring him again by closing her eyes, but when she dared open them again, because of his height, all she viewed were the snap buttons on his shirt. She had to bite her tongue to keep from reacting to the smooth skin at his collarbone.

Who on the planet, let alone in NYC, wore a partially unbuttoned, or in this case unsnapped, checkered western-style shirt, under a boot-length rain slicker, with nothing else to offer warmth? What a dolt. Okay, it was hot in the train, and mostly anywhere indoors, but a body still had to wander from place to place with exposure to the elements.

"So, cowboy, are you a marshal, or did you step out of some screenplay and stumble onto this train?"

"Could you repeat your earlier observation, ma'am?"

"What?"

"The part about how I smell good." The train jerked again, forcing them together, and she had no choice but to look up.

"Dammit."

"Ladies in New York City cuss, do they?"

"Oh, come on, did you get here by time machine? And yeah, ladies and not-so-ladylike gals—is that what you called me?" Kate tried to create some distance between them, but the crowded car forced her to remain his captive in too-close proximity.

"Come on, sugar, don't you see this is destiny?"

"Hell no. There is no effing destiny. Sugar, really? Step back. You're crowding me. I'm not sure what kind of fantasy world you're from but—"

"Texas. I can assure you, fifty thousand acres of ranchland peppered with prime beef, horse breeding, old trucks, dogs, and a bunkhouse full of sturdy cowhands ain't no fantasy." He grinned. "Well, wait a minute, come to think of it, that might be an uptight city girl's fantasy."

"Your fantasy, not mine, you ass." Shit, shit, shit, shit. She'd said that aloud.

"Maybe so. I like your powers of observation, ma'am, but I guess I ain't exactly sweeping you off your feet. Or—" he looked down past the edge of her coat, "those city slicker boots. Those shoes'll sink you up to your knees in cow manure on the ranch."

"Like that matters. I'll never set foot on your ranch. Whatever charm you may think you have, cowboy, for the record, it sucks. You're rude and might as well drive over my foot with a frigging tractor as soon as get my phone number. Dammit, now I even sound like you, you… cow-jerk." Kate turned and spun free, even as the train began to slow.

***

Cal saw tears sting her eyes, and he was willing to kick himself onto the third rail at that moment, except he had to stick around because there was something about the woman that grabbed his curiosity. Admittedly, he'd been pouring it on a little thick. What had she said? "Duh." Still, it gave him a kick to go all cowboy on people when he left the ranch on business. As for women, well, he'd been without one for a long time. He didn't count the occasional dalliance to keep sane, but even those had been few and far between since his wife left him for a financial management nerd. But Ms. Smell-Good Editor seemed special.

When she found out who he was—and she would—she'd have all rights to shoot him dead, right on the spot. It seemed stupid now, his idea to try to meet the book editor incognito.

The train screeched to a stop, and the doors opened. Cal didn't try to stop wet-coat girl, even when her last words stung.

"My stop, super jerk. Maybe you'll get run over by a stampede of fat shitty cows for Christmas." She twisted out of his grasp and disappeared in a crowd of commuters, leaving Cal to wonder if she was a natural redhead.

As he stepped onto the platform, his last thought was how much fun it would be to find out.

Chapter 2

Kate wasn't happy. If it wouldn't send her to the big house to live in a perpetual nightmare of orange, a color she despised, she'd borrow the cowboy from this morning, if she could find him—she'd have him shoot the smug coworker staring back across her desk.

"You want me to read that book?" She glanced at the manuscript Matt Andrews held, as he raised one eyebrow for emphasis. *Really? Almost all their submissions were electronic.* Of course, Matt knew her proclivity for editing the old fashioned way via pencil and a printed hard copy. "Which I get is my job, but a romance written by an unemployed, unheard-of writer who likely scribbled it out for the fun of it because he has boatloads of money—"

"By Jove, Kate, I think you've got it. For the record, he's not unemployed."

Matt's snarky reply pissed her off. The publishing world had its own set of rules, and murdering a fellow editor, not to mention her supervisor, wasn't allowed, even if justified. For some reason, it gave her comfort to slip one foot in and out of the shoes she'd changed into when she got to the office. She stared at him. "Why?"

"Because it's a great book." Matt's sometimes charming, other times—as in now—snide smile split his face into two bookend dimples. His hazel-hued eyes expressed the fun he was having at Kate's expense. "The characters are special. Let me rephrase that. Unique, compelling, happily ever after, but not until grief, conflict, tragedy, you name it, tortures the protagonist in a way that gets the reader, even you, to like men." The fingers of his left hand followed the crease of a pant leg. "I thought that might be a kind of religious experience for you."

"You're a shit."

"So it's rumored." He pushed the manuscript back across the smooth mahogany of her desk. She loved her desk, and especially loved the look of a maybe best seller sitting center stage on the polished wood. Her phone on the left, PC monitor to the right, a single steno pad with a pen clipped neatly onto one edge rested beneath the screen. No dust, no clutter, only the powerful brain of the computer humming quietly behind a magnetically latched door within the piece of furniture. She hated stuff that puttered around workstations like confused soldiers. Items like personalized coffee cups, paperclip dishes, pen holders, and those stackable sticky pads. It figured a higher power invented plugs and cords to annoy neat people.

Clutter meant distraction.

When Kate sat down to read any new asset, she locked the door. Sometimes she put on Mozart, other times she wanted no brain interference as she attacked the first few pages. If she were sent an electronic submission, a clerk made a print copy. Pages, from her first *Dick & Jane* primer to *Gone with the Wind,* mattered. She knew her reputation. Uptight, old-school-stick-in-the-mud, untouchable.

Old-fashioned or not, she adored paper, the smell of a book, and rereading a passage without scrolling up or down. More than that, she enjoyed the feel of a book in her hands, the anticipation of turning a page, including the occasional moistening of her fingertip. None of that mattered with an e-book. She didn't resent anybody who wanted to carry a tablet onto the subway and manage their work or leisure reading in such a convenient way. It wasn't Kate's way. You couldn't put a tablet over your face when you fell asleep at the beach.

"You owe me, Kate."

"Do I?" Her brain had been drifting. She'd been digging her toes into imaginary sand, a dangerous habit where Matt was concerned.

"We won't even argue the point, sweetheart. Read it, and then I'll set up a meeting between you, me, and the author next week." Matt stood, and despite the time spent sitting, his slack creases remained perfect. Like his hair, the space between piercing eyes, the straight nose, strong chin—perfect. And he knew it.

She studied Matt's expensive but understated attire. A lavender tie rested against a pale blue shirt that fit like canvas across a workout build, all framed by a professionally tailored navy-blue silk suit. His smug grin was back, and it pissed Kate off that she had been so weak and within days of starting her dream job as junior editor at Bennett & Willis.

Their first so-called dinner meeting, he'd had her in the sack. Romance, Kate's ass. Some of the staff hinted at it—that Kate had slept her way to the position she now held. Of course, how would anybody in the office know about the tryst? Matt the Mouth's behavior remained so freaking Neanderthal it exasperated Kate to think about it.

Worse, Matt thought he was great in bed, stellar, a hunk. She mentally slapped herself for faking *it* because it had only added to his ego. At least he hadn't called her a prude. The man sitting across from her no doubt carved notches of female conquests into his bedpost with his Mt. Blanc pen. And this despite the change in workplace philosophy and legal pressures from the courts. Too bad, but men like Matt still roamed office halls and bars like hungry lions on the Serengeti. She suspected that if Jake Willis had the real intel, Matt would be fired.

Kate also figured she hadn't been up to Matt's expectations, not enough to warrant a notch, and that hurt.

"You know, O'Malley," Matt's relentless grin returned, "you should get out more anyway. I mean, have you, uh, have you even had sex since our little…rendezvous how long now, two years ago?"

Kate didn't answer. Instead, she held up the middle finger of her left hand. Unladylike, crude, but satisfactory.

"A bit sensitive, Kate?"

For the first time since she'd been assigned her own office, Kate wished there *were* a few office-type items on her desk. Missiles to launch at Matt's head, like a hole punch, a stapler, or a hard copy of *War and Peace*. Absence of a weapon irritated Kate to the point of an uncontrolled blush. She felt the heat race up her neck to her forehead.

"You're cute pissed off, Katie. But I am right about the sex thing. Even the staff thinks you're too uptight to be effective."

Matt was lying, or so she hoped. Either way, restraint was no longer possible. "First of all, junior boss-man," she caught the tic in one cheek, *gotcha*, "don't ever call me Katie again. Second, you're a jerk, and your behavior is disgraceful, but I took part freely way back when. In fact I enjoyed it," *liar*, "a mutual romp for us both. But that is where it stops. I've earned my stripes here. Mr. Willis knows it, and I venture that if he knew about your behavior around the office, you'd be out."

"Whoa, missy, retract those claws. By the way, there's horses, trucks, and dogs in the book, plus, isn't a cowboy every woman's fantasy?"

"Oh boy. Horses. Gee, Matt, wow, oh my God, my interest is so totally peaked, horses, oh-boy-oh-boy." Kate wanted to clobber him. Instead, she capitulated in her head, and once that happened, there was no point in pushing Matt further. Oh, she might win in the end, but at a cost. So call her a major shrinking violet, she didn't care to go there. Not now, anyway.

"Touchy, touchy. Forget all this banter, Ms. O'Malley, read the book. That's the assignment from a senior editor. Period."

She bit her lip as he pushed the manuscript from the middle of her desk toward her hands. "Whatever."

Matt was almost out the door when he turned. "You should get laid, Kate."

The door closed behind him so that he didn't likely hear her oh-so-sensible shoe hitting square in the middle of the wood.

Chapter 3

Jake Willis waited for Kate O'Malley to pick up the phone. Unless she'd radically changed her work ethic—which meant a lightning strike, or an asteroid falling over Manhattan—Kate should be sitting at her desk alone, reading or editing.

And Jake? But for the call, he'd be wrapping presents and tussling with his youngest child. Ned, a not-quite-toddler, was a wobbly-walker this Christmas, but already intrigued by the idea of ribbons and wrapping. Soon he'd compete for the spot of top package shredder in competition with his older brothers, Jake Jr. and Eric 2. Uncertain how many toys were in the apartment's spare bedroom–each of which would require assembly in the next two weeks—he flipped the subject switch in his mind. Four fingers of good bourbon waited on the bar, but he had a call to make because of Lizzie.

Impossible to ignore Lizzie under any circumstance, but in seven years, Jake had come to understand his wife's determination and intuition when it came to the love lives of his employees or friends. In that respect, Lizzie might as well have been a Category 5 hurricane. Jake chuckled at the thought, no resentment in his heart or mind. In fact, for the second Mrs. Willis, her favorite holiday held a new tradition: matchmaking. Somehow, tortured and lonely souls crossed Lizzie's path, and presto, abracadabra, whatever Lizzie's magic, the couple wound up in love and married. Last year it was Trevor and Angie, a New York City police detective and their oldest child's schoolteacher. He grinned to himself at the recollection of his daughter, Samantha, and her involvement in her mother's efforts at making that match. In fact, in hindsight, Sam had played a small part in getting the Christmas romance of the year before the Trevor and Angie saga off the ground. That memorable machination involved another of Jake's editors, Eric Reynolds, and the now bestselling author Amy Grainger. That romance had resulted in his second son's name, Eric 2.

There wasn't always a method to Lizzie's madness, but then again, Amy and Eric were around a lot, and somehow, the "2" stuck, making it easy to yell for one or the other without confusion. Sam and Jake Jr. adopted it immediately. Once that happened, there was no turning back.

Sometimes Jake recalled the beauty of solitude, of being alone. He'd had it once, before Lizzie. Truth? He didn't miss it. But the year had passed, and Jake wondered when Lizzie would get to work on another two lovers unable to see their destiny. It shouldn't surprise him anymore, or ever for that matter. His life had morphed from near-bitter lonely widower to deeply-in-love-with-his-wife family man. He'd fallen the instant Lizzie stumbled into his arms, breaking her roommate's cherished slingbacks, spraining her ankle, and snaring his heart. All in a few heartbeats. Christmas—once the worst time of his life—had become the joyous season it was meant to be since Liz rocketed into Jake's world with a bestseller and a broken Jimmy Choo shoe.

"Hello?"

The ringing phone had become a live person, pulling him from reverie. "Kate, it's Jake Willis."

"Mr. Willis, hi. What's up?"

"Jake, Kate. Please, call me Jake."

"Sir…"

"No sir, either. Kate. Practice it in front of a mirror if you must. It's Jake."

"Okay, I guess."

"Did Matt Andrews give you that new book to read and consider in terms of acquiring the property?"

"Yes, but—"

"There's no 'but' about it, Kate. It's a Lizzie pick."

"Oh."

"Oh? Meaning Matt didn't tell you that Lizzie backed the writer's submission."

"No, sir. He did not. And I mean, Jake, sir."

He'd have to accept the concession that "Jake, sir" might be the best he could get until his newest full editor got her initiative up.

"Yes, well, it would be a favor to me if you'd read the book and give me feedback."

"Sir?"

"Jake, Kate, Jake, please."

"I'll try, sir, Jake…"

"To clarify. Yes, you'll read the book?"

"Yes, sir."

He let the sir go. "Good."

"Mr. Willis?"

"Yes, Kate?" He bit back the exasperation at trying to get his editor to be more familiar in communicating.

"It's not my area of—"

"Jake Willis, is that work on the phone?"

He turned in response to his wife's question, not bothering to cup a hand over the receiver. "It's Kate O'Malley."

"Oh, good. Hand over." Lizzie plopped the child on her arm into Jake's lap, exchanging a squirming Ned Willis for the telephone receiver. "Hi, Kate? It's Liz Willis. Hang on. I'm putting you on speaker, no secrets in this house. Do you have any plans for tomorrow?"

"Housecleaning and then work."

"Tomorrow is Saturday, Kate."

"I know, Mrs. Willis, but I've a new book to review and—"

"Yes, *The Christmas Bargain*, I know. I loved it, but it can't come out until next year now, and I need your help on something."

Jake almost burst out laughing. His wife's help on something meant only one thing. She had a plan that involved love, Kate O'Malley, and who? Whom? It didn't matter much about the form of the word, Lizzie was up to something, and he could only wonder what poor male was destined to become the "y" in the "x" + equation.

"Well, I need to take the kids to see Santa tomorrow. It's a joy that won't last forever. In fact, Samantha—you've met Sam in the office, haven't you—is already aware Santa is sort of a fake. She likes the idea of a jolly old elf though, so she's willing to play along for the boys. It's close with Jake Jr. He's not as obtuse as his dad, but at least as skeptical." Liz grinned at Jake. "Eric's okay at four-something, well, that's my math. Anyway, taking all four children is difficult, especially with Ned verging on his terrible twos." Ned, oblivious to the conversation, giggled in Jake's lap, drooling happily as his father clapped two small hands together in a patty-cake game. He'd save spanking Liz for the cut until later.

"You need me to babysit or something?"

"Well, more like accompany me. I have a few things that need arrangements for pickup by December twenty-second. I hoped you could stand in line with the kids in case there's any delay. I mean there shouldn't be, as most schools aren't out until next weekend. Anyway, it wouldn't be like I would leave you alone with my three terrorists and an in-diapers baby for long. Plus, Sam is good at keeping her brothers in tow. After that, I hoped we'd grab a bite, my treat. I'd like to pick your brain a little—oh, I know you haven't read the book yet—but maybe I could help with the few issues I noted in *The Christmas Bargain*. That way you'd know what to look for, along with your terrific editing, of course."

Jake bit his tongue. When Lizzie was on a roll, a smart person got out of the way. And he also now had a good guess who Lizzie thought was the perfect HEA for his editor.

"Mrs. Willis—"

"Liz."

"Well, Mrs. Will…Liz, you're a great writer, and frankly, I'd be a little intimidated."

"That's silly. Will you do it? Please?" Jake looked up at his wife and rolled his eyes. He mouthed the words "I know what you're up to, Lizzie" but she waved him off.

"I don't know if I'm much good with kids, maybe in an apartment with toys, cartoons, cookies, and giant locks on the door, but in a department store?"

Liz chuckled. "You're funny, Kate. No wonder Jake sings your praises. It takes a good sense of humor to edit contemporary romance. Well, that's my opinion, anyway. How about we meet at the entrance of Santa's Village, say eleven a.m. tomorrow? That way I can have the kids strapped into chairs and ordering food before they get cranky and tired. "

Jake knew the short silence that followed was his editor calculating the odds of saying no. There'd be no repercussions from her boss, and he felt she knew that. He also knew Lizzie could apply subtle pressure that made a person wonder if they'd forgotten their deodorant that morning, or if there was a mustard stain on a lapel or tie.

"Okay. I guess. I mean, it would be great to get feedback from you about the book."

"Perfect. It's casual of course. You don't have to show up in editor garb." Lizzie winked at Jake.

"Okay."

"Great, tomorrow then. And are you at the office? Well, Jake says go home, you work too hard."

"Thank you, Mrs. Willis."

"Liz."

"Okay. Bye."

Jake held his breath until the phone was cradled. "You're up to something, Elizabeth Callahan Willis."

"Jake, I'd like to get to know Kate, at least more than a casual office meet and greet. And besides, I think the kids will love her not to mention she's alone here in the city, right?"

"Right, as she's been for two years. But the good Lord knows we can't have that now, can we, Lizzie?"

"Damn straight, Mr. Willis, sir. Damn straight."

Liz spun and handed Jake the whiskey he'd poured twenty minutes earlier. "You deserve this, JW. You want me to take Ned off your hands?"

"I'm fine, and he's practically asleep."

"Right, and that'll last." Kissing the top of his head, she turned toward the far end of the apartment. "I'm ordering for Friday pizza night. Sam chose cheese, cheese, and extra cheese. To be clear, 'no stinky fish, Mom.'"

"Well, at least I'll know whatever something fishy you're cooking up, Mrs. Willis, it won't be the smell of our pizza." The laughter he loved filled the room as his wife headed down the hall to find Jake Jr., Eric 2, and Sam. He would feel sorry for his newest editor except for the fact that Lizzie was, well, Lizzie.

With his wife's mind made up, there'd be little help for those swept up in the plan.

Chapter 4

Kate scowled down at her phone. *Traitor. What did you make me agree to?* She was petrified at the idea of spending a few hours with the wife and children of the Willis of Bennett & Willis Publishing. *I mean, who has four kids these days?*

She thought about packing her bags and flying to Bermuda for the holidays. Of course, even the notion of such an adventure was absurd. Kate was anything but irresponsible. That, and she hated flying. Maybe a road trip to Vermont would do

Except she didn't own a car anymore and hadn't since she moved to New York City.

Oh well, there was nothing to do for it now. Tapping a pencil against the manuscript calmed her nerves. Most of the staff had left except for some folks in the mail department, and Jenny Carnes who'd volunteered to get the office Christmas tree up and ready for decorating.

Jake Willis encouraged all faiths and practices to be reflected in the office. Hanukah was well represented, even though it was later this year, as was Kwanzaa. Any conceivable celebration during December was allowed equal wall and shelf space.

Kate stood up to release some of her nervous energy, leaning against the door frame to study her publishing world. Two big suites, one for Mr. Willis and the other for Bob Bennett, had windows that looked out on the work floor. Everything was dark now, but during the day, the publishing world was on full display. Kate could see if there were meetings or animated discussions about a project, and it didn't matter what the reason, she loved every aspect. It reminded Kate of newsrooms in old movies. Her cubby was in a corner, so she could see some of the office with the door all the way open, but once she closed herself in, it seemed a cocoon. Too bad that safe feeling could be disrupted any time, most often by Matt.

She stretched, hopeful that getting her blood moving might inspire a continued push to get through the book. Kate had managed fifteen pages of the mandatory reading and had to admit it was well-written. But the characters would have pulled her in without it going hot and heavy on page one. She remained uncomfortable that clothes were already flying off by page three. Kate would prefer to believe it didn't happen like that, but she supposed it did. She'd been there and would never allow herself to be in that situation again. A mental flash of that awful night with Matt Andrews crashed her solitude. A romance novel should be tension without wet, slobbering sex. Maybe she truly was a dinosaur.

Hating it didn't change the fact that sex sold.

Right, Kate, that's a never-before-made observation. Not even close to astute.

As soon as she started Chapter Two, the fatigue settled in her bones. She couldn't fight a changing world. Resigned, she slipped the manuscript into her briefcase and headed for home. Her loneliness made the book heavier. Catching an image of herself in the darkened office windows, she tried to straighten out the slump that often settled on her frame at the day's end.

***

Geeze, what did I do last night? An empty bottle of Chardonnay was still on the coffee table, and one Smurf slipper sat next to it, along with the tray from a diet frozen-turkey dinner. She'd fallen asleep on the sofa with the heater on, which explained the stuffed-up nose, unpleasant breath, and the worst hairdo ever—a fact she knew without the help of a mirror. The needlepoint pillow she'd slept on was wet with drool.

"What time is it?" Of course, nobody was there to respond, but the blinking light on her answering machine set off warning signals. Kate wobbled up from the couch, teetered over to the bar that separated the functional kitchen from dining/living, and punched the button on her beloved, old-fashioned machine.

"Kate? Hi, it's Liz Willis. I can't believe you have an answering machine, but sure glad you do—your cell went straight to voicemail. The kids and I are leaving the apartment in about thirty-five minutes. Can't wait to see you at the entrance to Santa's Village. Hope you had a good night, any chance you read a few chapters of the book? Okay, never mind. See you soon."

The message timestamp was 9:52 a.m.

"Shit." She looked at the clock on the range. 10:05 a.m. She'd slept through four rings and Liz's message. "Holy shit." Nobody could argue that Kate O'Malley had the spirit of Christmas in her heart, what with her frequent use of the word "holy." And late was late. Even if it were a babysitting job, and even though Liz Willis was not the boss, she was the boss's wife. Kate's internal rulebook would not tolerate a no-show or extremely late appearance.

"If you're not early, Kate, you're late." Again, there was nobody in her apartment, or life for that matter, to suggest she had once more made a brilliant assessment regarding time. *Dr. Hawking, look out.*

That Kate was doing a favor for Liz Willis didn't diminish the importance of the scheduled meeting. *And why is it so important?*

Kate had a feeling there was another agenda, and her boss might even be in on it. Or at least complacent about the reason, the real reason Liz was so adamant about meeting at the entrance to a department store's Santa Land or whatever it was called. Her thoughts followed Kate into the bathroom, where the mirror she relied on to get out the door each morning, an object that was never kind, let her have it.

"Oh, for Pete's sake, Kate. You look like shit." Okay, Santa could go ahead and put her on the naughty list, because right now, she didn't give a rat's behind.

One half of her face was pitted with the pillow's pattern, and the math for getting to the store on time left her little more than thirty minutes to be out the door. She could add five or ten for the time it took a mom to get three children into caps, boots, etc. She had no clue how long one needed to get a toddler together. That might even be impossible. Kate had never been a mom, and she didn't know Mrs. Willis. Once in the office, maybe a few words at last year's Christmas party, and then the phone call.

She turned the shower to cold and stepped under the water. The shock helped clear her brain a little as Kate recalled office talk. Not gossip, but genuine stuff about what an amazing human being Liz Callahan, the writer, and Liz Callahan Willis, the wife, could be, including her kindnesses to writers and editors alike. Disconcerting were the rumors that Mrs. Willis was something of a matchmaker.

"Shit. No, it can't be." *So, on the naughty list for my language. Sorry, Santa.*

She twisted the handle off and grabbed a towel, pondering things she'd heard over the past two years. Fretting was a waste of time, and mentally kicking herself into gear, Kate focused on getting herself in tune with what might be Liz Willis's timing. There had to be twenty minutes minimum to get that many non-adults into a cab or a subway.

"Oh hell. They must have a town car. I can't even count on a delay for mass transit. Shit." As usual, the emptiness of her apartment offered little advice.

Tangled hair brushed back with rigorous and unkind strokes now bounced behind her head in an acceptable ponytail. It was a bit severe, but she compensated by putting in sparkly Christmas tree earrings, a dab of amber eyeshadow, a single brushstroke of mascara, and her lightly tinted moisturizer. Her gloss would be in her coat pocket. She'd already pulled on her plaid mid-calf skirt, a green turtleneck, and brown leather boots.

She took a last look in the floor-length mirror. "Damn, you look okay…I guess." Well, she didn't need to impress the kids, only Liz Willis. Knowing anything that happened, and how well lunch went, whether Kate killed one of the kids or something, would all get back to Jake through his wife's eyes. That little scrap of knowledge was the scary part.

Bennett & Willis was her employer, her life. There was office talk, the story of the Liz and Jake legend. Her boss hadn't merely suffered when his first wife died in the South Tower on 9/11. He'd been bitter and alone, but functioning. Kate thought you could be so skilled at deflecting emotion that a person could operate on autopilot. He'd spent eight years of living without life in his veins, so the rumors went. And then came the story of a manuscript in a pizza box. Jake and Liz had met, had a whirlwind romance, and now here they were. Four kids, eight years later, in love.

Damn, I need to focus. Keys in hand, shoulder bag snug against her donned Navy wool coat, and Kate was out the door at 10:28 a.m.

Chapter 5

Kate was late. As she waited, Liz had Ned in one arm with Jake Jr. and Eric 2's small hands looped through the belt at her waist. Sam had secured herself to the handle on Ned's diaper bag. *Check. All kids present and functioning.* Despite feeling like a porter at Grand Central station, Liz was happy. She never lost sight of the miracle her children represented. That Jake Willis had fallen for her, lock, stock, and craziness, never stopped vibrating through her skin.

Still, she was a bit surprised that Kate wasn't here yet. The girl emanated a calm, serious…well, in fact, a stern exterior, and she *lived* at the office. Jake had never mentioned his editor being late to meetings, which was one of his pet peeves. Well, it had been anyway. Things changed a little with child number three.

Liz knew one thing in her heart. Kate was lonely, fearful, and somewhere along the way, her heart had foreclosed on any hope of love.

And then there was Caleb Walker. Delicious. Of course, Liz's eyes would never wander. She loved Jake, period. That included all the molecules and atoms that made up the man. But dang if the rancher from north Texas didn't have it all, including money and talent. His looks? Like he'd climbed right out of the pages of a book into real life. Chiseled, rugged, blue-eyed—sort of. The last time she'd met with Walker, his eyes had seemed more gray than blue. Where was she? Oh, the facial hair. Their newest writer sported a one-day beard that might have landed him on the cover of *The Great Outdoors.*

Handsome and bitter, sexy, alone, and brilliant. Enter Kate O'Malley. Oblivious, it seemed, to the fact of her beauty.

"Mrs. Willis?"

Liz did a half-spin. Sam, like a pilot-fish, made it in turn, Ned gurgled, while Jake Jr., who had taken Eric's hand, stood his ground staring at the entrance to see Santa.

"Oh, Kate. Yeah. So glad you made it. Santa will be on his legendary throne shortly."

"Hello, Ms. O'Malley, I'm Sam. Wow, you have red hair and green eyes too. "

Kate looked down at the first Willis child, and Liz noted the somewhat shocked expression on Kate's face. Samantha Willis stood before Liz's next project with perfect posture, her hand out for a formal introduction. Until a year or so ago, Sam's hair was fire-engine red, and now it was more carrot-like, but all three of them had green eyes and freckles. It might have caused anyone to do a double take. "Samantha Willis, manners."

"Did I interrupt? Golly, I didn't mean to, not with…" Sam's eyes widened, but with an "I get it" grin, "the elves, you know, watching." She turned her face up to Liz, "Gosh, Mom, it's like we could be the three Musketeers, right? Except the Musketeers were French, and I'm half-Irish." She turned her smile back on Kate. "Are you Irish, Ms. O'Malley?"

"Well, Irish roots, yes. And I guess we could be Musketeers, at least for today. " Kate held out her hand. "Nice to be formally introduced, Ms. Willis."

"Oh, you have to call me Sam, it's a rule."

"A rule?"

"Yes." Sam turned her face up to Liz. "Right, Mommy?"

Liz always got a lump in her throat, remembering how Jake's first wife was the namesake of their firstborn. Liz had never once felt uncomfortable that she and Jake named their daughter after Samantha. "Yes, baby. It's a rule." Turning back to their lunch date, she said, "Kate?"

"Ready and able, Mrs. Wil— Liz. At least I think so."

Jake's employee still looked befuddled, but Liz counted on Sam, who could talk chrome off a bumper, to fill in any blanks Kate might have. "Great. The line starts, well," she juggled Ned and pointed her index fingers at an "x" on the linoleum floor, "here, we're in it. Santa should show up in about," she glanced at her watch, "oh, three minutes? The store is profoundly serious about scheduling. I need to run down to shipping as I explained. Uh, well, this is a little awkward, but Sam can manage her younger brother, and Jake Jr. in turn will keep a grip on Eric 2. I am sure you're nervous, don't be. Then there's Ned…"

"Ned?"

"Well, you have to hold Ned until it's his turn to drool and bubble in Santa's lap." Liz tried her world-famous smile on Jake's youngest editor. "Then you kind of hand him off, close up and personal like."

"Mrs. Willis?"

Liz had to bite the inside of her cheek not to burst out laughing at the look of terror and uncertainty on her husband's employee's face. "It's okay, Kate, you'll be fine. Sam will help you through it. This is her fifth year of visits on her own two feet as we don't count the first two years. Um, I don't think Santa will ask you to sit in his lap, but you never know."

"Oh my."

"Samantha Willis, front and center."

"Yes, supreme ruler."

"Okay, Sam, knock it off, that kind of thing will scare Kate."

"Nah, Mom, it won't. Kate has the coolest boots, she can kick 'em in the knees, right?" Kate's baffled expression deserved some explanation.

"I'm sorry, Kate. There's an old cheer, 'rah-rah-ree, kick 'em in the knee, rah-rah-mutt, uh, kick 'em in the…other knee—our version anyway."

"I've never heard that."

"Don't give it a second thought. And it's Liz, remember? I'll be back as soon as I can." She dashed to the elevator. Shipping was two floors down, and she needed to make arrangements for the American Girl dolls to be delivered by the twenty-second. She glanced back as the doors started to close. "You can do it, Kate."

***

The image of Liz waving, with a big grin on her face as the elevator closed, created more anxiety for Kate. Rah-rah-what? Anything, no, everything could go wrong, and with three young children and a not-quite-a-toddler in her charge, who could blame her for being petrified? Ned chose that moment to spit up on Kate's coat, and Jake Jr. started to tell his brother, Eric 2, that the elves knew he'd been a terrible little boy and so there was no point in talking to Santa. Tears were already spilling down bright red cheeks, with Eric 2 on the verge of wailing. Kate needed to ask Liz about the added modifier to Eric's name, but for now she had to figure out how to keep the boy from a tantrum. She patted his head. "It's going to be okay, Eric, Jake made that up." His tears had stopped, but the third Willis child looked terrified.

Sam, caught up in the excitement of Santa despite having turned seven sometime in the last two months, hopped up and down because the elf himself entered with a deep-voiced ho-ho-ho, and settled onto his big-jolly-old-elf chair.

Shit and triple times a train wreck. How had Kate managed to get herself into this impossible situation?

Chapter 6

Kate couldn't hear much of Sam's wish list from her spot in line. And it didn't matter because she was holding her breath against the smell of Ned's baby vomit on her right shoulder. Jake Jr. held her hand in a vise grip, his eyes bright with anticipation, and Eric 2, having overcome the crummy mocking from his older brother, clutched her skirt with both small hands, scrunching the fabric into knots.

Kate hadn't prayed to anyone or anything in ten-plus years, but in the last five minutes, she'd tossed up a plea for help to every saint listed in her way-back memories of childhood. But her pleas weren't working. Santa hadn't disappeared, Sam still sat on one of his knees, and the Willis children were still in Kate's charge. By the animated yet matter-of-fact way in which Sam unfurled a scroll of wishes onto Santa's red velvet lap, you'd never have thought she'd had doubts about the elf. There seemed little doubt that the Willis determination had been transferred to the delightful little girl. "And one more thing, Mr. Claus…"

"Yes, Sam?" Santa's voice had multiple levels of deep and sexy tones, but Kate remained unimpressed. Still, when the hired store Santa laughed, it floated above the crowd of anxious, weary, and otherwise impatient parents, catching Kate's attention each time he barked a ho-ho-ho. The man who captivated Sam was a big fake. Did anyone truly buy into this crap? She didn't discount faith, or people believing in something, but all that stuff—Santa, the miniature sled, reindeer, little toy horns—what the hell did it all mean? Her childhood had been a hollow echo of any such joy. For crying out loud, the internet alone was sufficient cause to dismiss the elf.

"And I have a new friend. Her name's Ms. O'Malley."

At the sound of her name, Kate snapped to attention. A giggling Sam Willis seemed to be sharing Kate's presence with the bearded man. It forced her mind front and center.

"Is she here? Your new friend."

"Oh yes, Santa." The small but straight index finger of Sam's right hand pointed down the stairs to Kate. The boys remained oblivious to anything but Santa, his elves, and all the surrounding toys. Ned had switched to chewing on her shirt. "She's right there, holding my little brother, Ned, and those are my other brothers hanging on to Kate's skirt." Sam identified the boys with an exaggerated sigh. "Jake Jr. and Eric 2."

"Ah, I see her."

"Well, my mom says that Ms. O'Malley needs something very, very, very special from Santa."

"Really?"

Kate had heard enough. "Santa, can we get the line moving here? I'm having trouble, as I'm sure a lot of other folks are, keeping the children patient."

Sam pleaded, "No, Kate, I'm almost done. I'm asking Santa about Mommy's wish."

The request might seem reasonable to a mother or an actual babysitter, but Kate was neither. And whatever "Mommy's wish" might have been, Kate didn't have a clue because Sam scaled Santa's suit like an expert mountain climber and whispered in his ear.

If she knew the children better, if she had more confidence in her ability to manage the boss's kids, Kate would have stomped up to the platform and grabbed Sam by the collar of her adorable velvet dress. But the girl was done, and sliding off good old St. Nick's lap, she strode like some wish-warrior down the five steps to the two green-clad elves, who were waving cellophane-wrapped candy canes, and coupons for the toy department. *Talk about marketing.*

Kate had to fulfill her promise to Liz Willis, so she nudged Jake toward the platform with a determined, "You go on, Jake, and take Eric with you, but please remember there are a lot of children who want to talk to Santa. It would be rude to take too much of his time." There was no response, and she hadn't expected one.

Jake bounded up the stairs, Eric in tow, and leapt onto Santa's fake belly. Kate stifled a burst of laughter at Santa's "oof." It served the fraud right. Admittedly, the store's representative of the North Pole had a storybook sparkle in his eyes. She took a longer look.

Something—she couldn't peg it—about Santa seemed vaguely familiar.

The store elf had helped Eric 2 onto his other knee, scooting the boy against his chest. Jake Jr. resettled himself on the jolly fat man's lap. *Fat my ass*, crossed Kate's mind as she held on to a now-very-ripe baby Ned, simultaneously scanning the crowd for the return of Liz Willis.

***

"Who do we have here? Do you know who I am?"

"'Course I do, Mr. Santa." Jake giggled, stretched out his legs, and clicked the toes of his winter boots together. "I'm Jake Willis Jr. and that's one of my brothers, Eric 2."

Eric burped, and Santa laughed, turning back to his older brother. "Eric 2?"

"That's 'cause we know another Eric."

"I see. And how old are you, Master Jake?"

"I'm not a master. I'm a boy. And I want a new train that runs around the Christmas tree on account of I kinda broke last year's train. It still runs but there's bumps in some of the tracks. Also, a real bicycle with training wheels and a baby sister to keep my other sister busy." He rolled his eyes at the ceiling, "She bosses me around, and I'm almost six."

Caleb had thought Sam Willis had the market on impossible gifts. The job of Santa had become a challenge Cal didn't expect. And now he had a living example of a way-too-smart kid squirming in his lap. Meanwhile, a shy version of Jake Jr. sat on his other knee. Still, since the day after Thanksgiving, Cal had heard a request for sophisticated electronic toys and computer tablets. Nice that the kid wanted a baby sister even if the request might be a bit self-centered, not to mention impossible.

He was thinking it too bad that nobody in New York had asked for a pony when Jake Jr. tugged on his sleeve. "Have you been a good boy?" Caleb asked.

"The best. Even my sister, Sam… you met Sam. She concurred." Cal did a double take, while Jake Jr. added, "Concurred. We have to learn one big word a day, or Mom says we're toast." Cal laughed, a real laugh, but he made it sound ho-ho-ho-ish, like a true North Pole resident, before he paused to let the boy in his lap continue. "And Sam told you a secret wish."

"She did, and as Santa Claus, you must know I can't divulge her request, even if you torture me."

Jake Jr's eyes widened, "What's a deevulge? Is it like a shovel?"

The girl in charge of the Willis children laughed, and the sound of it captured a piece of Cal's heart. Too bad he couldn't reveal himself, but after yesterday's subway encounter, that was a bad idea.

"Anyway, I don't need a shovel, and my sister's a little silly."

"So, young man, whatever would you want another sister for?"

"I told you, Sam is a girl, and girls like girls, and my mom likes kids. A lot."

"Is that your mom in line right there?" Cal knew the answer but was enjoying the interaction with the small boy.

"Nope. That's my dad's employee. Dad makes books, but I'm not allowed to read them. It's big kids' stuff."

"I see." Cal shifted the boy to relieve the numbness creeping into his thigh. He also tried to make eye contact with the girl. Well, she was a woman, but he couldn't stop himself from thinking something about her remained childlike. It was obvious she was struggling with the assignment of watching three children and a toddler. As Santa, he'd seen Kate in line from behind the display's workshop. He didn't have to guess she was the editor assigned to review his submission, because Liz Willis had set the whole Santa-visit thing up, and then there had been the subway. It was mostly coincidence that he'd run into her on the subway.

Mostly.

He guessed he'd been a bad boy, because he'd asked Bennett & Willis staff when Kate arrived at work, and they were all too willing to share the fact that Kate O'Malley was a creature of habit. Liz had provided greater details. But he hadn't known he'd be attracted to the timid editor. He let Jake Jr. chatter on about baby sisters and space rockets. At least until Eric 2 burped.

Cal turned to Jake Jr.'s brother. "Do you know what you want for Christmas, Eric?"

The younger boy answered with a fit of giggles, so his brother interceded. "He wants a new trike. He could have mine when I get a real bike, but Mom says it's good for a boy to have his first three-wheeler."

"That's wise. I'll make a note to the elves not to shortchange Eric because there's already one trike in the house. Anything else?"

"Eric likes to fart in the bathtub, so some floaty things are good." Cal bit his tongue, wondering if the editor-babysitter heard the request, but she seemed occupied with the toddler in her arms. What was with the severe ponytail? She reminded him a little of a slim Barbie doll. He chuckled to himself about thinking of her anatomical attributes, whatever these might be. There was no way of telling given the thick wool coat she continued to sport—a coat he'd already met up close and personal.

Anyway, he couldn't be blamed for setting up the subway thing. He'd had no idea that Liz Willis would call later to tell him about the scheme to get Kate here to meet jolly old Santa Caleb. Still, whatever Liz was cooking up didn't change what had happened between Cal and Kate when he'd forced his way into her space on the train. The encounter, at least from his view, was hot. Too hot to ignore, but also absurd to pursue. He shook off the thoughts, because if anyone knew what he was thinking while in his role as Santa Claus? He'd spend Christmas in jail.

"So, Jake Jr., do you have any other requests, like, oh, say, electronic games?"

"Well, I have an Xbox, but it already has lots of games and Mom says I should make my horzons bigger."

"Horizons."

"Sure, that."

"Well, good for your mom. And the lady who brought you here, does she want anything?" Caleb tried to get the girl in the winter coat to look his way. "If you know, that is."

"Oh, well, I don't, but Mommy told my dad that she needs love."

Caleb suppressed a grin trying to force its way onto his face. "Well, well—maybe I'll get a letter from her with a wish list, but now I need to see some more children, don't you think?"

"Absopositive. I'm not supposed to stay up here too long on account of sharing being a golden rule."

"Your mom's right, but isn't the word absopositively?" Cal was having fun, even if nobody in Texas would believe being a department store Santa could chip away at his bitter side.

"Oh Santa, it can't be."

"Okay, I'm curious. Why?"

"Because absopositively is adverb abuse."

"Ah." Cal was officially in like with his mentor, Liz. "Okay. Now keep an eye out for my elves and be a good boy. Ho, ho, ho."

"Thanks, Santa. Bye." Jake jumped down, helping Eric 2 off Santa's lap. He turned on the last step. "I forgot to ask. Santa, do you want anything special for Christmas?"

"Ho, ho, ho. No thanks, Jake Jr. I have everything I need at the North Pole." His hoped-for publisher's two middle children scampered down the ramp toward the elves, who hadn't wavered in their commitment to hand out discounts and candy.

For no reason, a thought struck Cal. *I have everything I need, but nothing I want.*

And then it dawned he knew what he wanted after all. It was the stern-looking, vulnerable, schoolmarm-like book editor, Kate O'Malley. His neck flushed from heat as she approached with yet another Willis offspring. *It has to be the beard and the polyester suit.* But he recognized the symptoms. Pure desire for the proper woman wrapped up like a chrysalis in a wool coat simmered his blood.

That he wanted to free the woman from the tight ponytail, the coat, the strict-dress-code look, wanted her to be the girl who cried out for ecstasy on those first pages of his book, surprised Caleb J. Walker. He'd long ago given up the idea of love. But he was certain he wanted Kate, the subway girl. He also realized he needed her to want him, and that was a first. He put the brakes on his jump-in brain. One thing was more important to him than a romp with any woman, and that was to get his first novel published. Still, the conflict between his two desires left Cal uncertain.

***

Was it wrong? Wrong to want to drop an eighteen-month-old baby on the steps to Santa Claus? To desert her charges and bolt for the underwear department, or curse her boss's wife for leaving Kate alone in Christmas Village to face a fake-fat Santa with laughing eyes? And how come Santa had a tan?

It was insane that Kate was standing in this line to begin with, in charge of her boss's four—count them—*four* children, and scheduled to have lunch with that same boss's wife. How the freakin' Christmas-movie shit was this all coming together, while a little boy squirmed and burbled out milky dribble for a third time in twenty minutes onto Kate's best wool coat? A wool coat she couldn't extricate herself from because of holding on to Ned Willis. The store temperature had ramped up in the time she'd held her place in line, and she could feel the small drops of perspiration on her brow.

"Well, ma'am," Santa's Texas-resonance rang yet another bell in Kate's mind, "are you going to let me hold that boy and see what he'd like for Christmas, or are you here for a wish list of your own?"

"Back off, Santa-boy." Kate's serious tone was hushed by her concern that even a baby might catch her angry vibe. "Ned is not my child, but he would like to drool on your red coat. In my dreams, he'd baby-upchuck on that lovely white fur."

"Ho, ho, ho." Gloved hands reached for the boy in her arms, and she trusted in the store's vetting process enough to release Ned to the lying sack of Santa ho-ho-ho-ing his way into the holiday season.

With another ho-ho-ho, she was certain the Santa cooing to little Ned was the very man who'd held her captive on the subway. Oh sure, the suit and beard were a clever cover-up, but there was no mistaking the eyes. No forgetting the same laugh lines that put him in his late thirties, even early forties.

Dammit. He was sort of cute as Santa, but he'd been plain hot on that train.

"So, Ned's mom?"

His not-so-Santa voice was another tell. "I'm not Ned's mom, but you know that, and since you haven't been formally introduced to the boy, you've clearly got some inside intel."

"Well, I'm Santa, not-Ned's-mom. I've got elves everywhere, so as the song says, you'd better watch out."

"Right."

"I'm also an acquaintance of Mrs. Willis. You know this baby's wet, right?"

"True Santa question that." Kate glared at him.

"Sure is, been here since the day after Thanksgiving and I've had my fair share of stinky diapers and wet jodhpurs."

"'Jodhpurs'? You are the weirdest department store Santa I've ever met."

"You could come up here and tell me what you want for Christmas, not-Ned's-mom. I have an extra knee."

Kate sputtered, as no snappy comeback materialized on her lips. And that pissed her off. Totally. Plus, the Texas-accent rang truer when he became a smart-ass. Which might mean he had a guard to let down. With a little more time, she'd bet a pair of spurs she could topple his ego with some witty cut.

"Kate, goodness, I'm sorry that took so long."

Was it long? Not really, only a lifetime.

Liz came up to the second step next to Kate and looked around. "Where are the kids?"

Shit, shit, shit. In sparring with the cowpuncher, she'd lost the Willis children.

"Here, Mom," Sam piped up from a fenced partition next to Santa's Toy Shop. Jake Jr. stood beside his sister, the evidence of what remained of a free candy cane pink and sticky around his mouth. Eric 2 sat on the floor, rubbing his candy cane across the carpet. There was no escape from the area with the curly-slippered elves acting as centurions at the gate.

"Hi, kiddos. Hello, Santa." Liz skipped up the remaining steps to Santa's throne, scooping the small boy into her arms. "Oh yuck." A true mom, she double-checked her instincts by a pull at the elastic of Ned's pants waist. "I'm going to have to manage this, Santa."

Kate stared dumbfounded as Santa laughed aloud, then winked at Liz. "So, a delay on lunch?"

"Not much, Mr. Claus." Liz looked over her shoulder. "Besides, it appears you will have a riot if you don't see another dozen children."

Kate hadn't noticed before, but Santa's helpers had put up a sign about eight or nine sets of parents back. "Santa will Return at 1 p.m. The reindeer need feeding." Cute, but if she were having lunch with Kate and the children, why would Santa be joining them?

"Liz?"

"Oh, Kate, you're a dear. I'm going to take Jake Jr., Eric, and Ned to the restroom. That candy cane face is disgusting." Liz rubbed her older son's head. "And we can't sit through lunch, even if it is a cafeteria, with Ned's diaper this ripe." Liz turned to Sam. "Sweetheart, can you keep track of Kate for me, and help her find the cafeteria? I think we're still early enough for them to give you a table with five big-people chairs and two high chairs."

"Sure, Mom." Sam grinned from ear to ear. "And I'll ask about a booster seat for Jake Jr."

"Of course. Do you need a booster seat, Sam?"

"Well, I'll try the chair first and then ask Kate. If she can only see my eyes across the table, then she can get me the booster."

"You're my funny monster, Samantha Willis."

Sam giggled, taking Kate's hand. "We gotta go, Ms. O'Malley."

"Kate is okay, Sam."

"Goodie. But we still need to beat everybody to the cafeteria."

Liz headed for the restrooms, and Sam tugged Kate in the direction of the escalator, explaining as they went that the moving stairs were "totally awesome."

As they headed down to the mezzanine, Kate bent to capture Sam's attention and tapped on the girl's shoulder. "Honey, why five big-people chairs?"

Sam's smile was nothing compared to the conspiratorial sparkle in her eyes. "It's a secret."

"Sam?" Kate tried a stern tone.

"Because," holding up one hand, Sam counted off by folding her fingers down one at a time, "You...me...Mommy...Jake with a booster seat..." The little girl was down to her thumb, which she held up above her head, "and Santa." The child nearly collapsed with laughter.

Kate looked straight ahead, waiting for the last step of the moving staircase to fold into the bottom platform, taking her with it. She realized she'd interpreted Liz's comment to store Santa correctly. *I'm having lunch with Santa.* Quadruple shit. She should work on her abuse of the English language, even if it were only in her head. But this planned luncheon had all the earmarks of plotting, manipulation, and even treachery.

Chapter 7

Jake Jr. hummed while pushing chicken nuggets cut in the shape of elf hats around a plate smeared with ketchup and fries. Eric 2 had taken two bites of a hot dog and now seemed to be in a stare-down with the thing. Sam was explaining every sight and sound of Santa's Village to her mother. Her hands gesticulated in terms of height and weight, describing colors and making sounds as if she were on a stage recounting the morning to thousands, instead of her younger siblings, mother, and a new acquaintance. Little Ned seemed content to watch Liz's gold bangles reflect the light each time she raised a forkful of Cobb salad toward her mouth.

The conversation to this point had been dominated by the excited children, first about ordering, then about being hungry, and after a few bites of each of their meals, Jake Jr. joined in. To Kate's annoyance, the kid touted Santa at the table as the wonderfulest, bestest, and funnest ever of all time.

As far as Jake's admiration for cowboy-Santa, Kate didn't agree. The man, red suit and beard or not, in her view, was a jackass. Now that she was sure the children's Santa was the same man who'd accosted her on the subway yesterday morning, she was disturbed that a reputable department store may have hired a sex offender.

Vetted or not, does anybody know the guy? Ted Bundy got away with murder on his charm. Kate shook off her dark thoughts and returned her attention to Sam's ongoing monologue about the amazing Mr. Claus. In contrast to Kate's limited in-head and not-so-complimentary vocabulary, it was difficult not to notice Sam's articulate delivery of the visit. All the chatter in Kate's head was giving her a pain behind her temples. She decided to let it go for now. But that didn't mean her observations about the store Santa would be checked like a coat at La Bernardin.

Settling into her blackened chicken salad, Kate chewed on a spicy bite, wishing for a beer to put out the fire in her mouth. Not five seconds passed before she realized it wasn't a cool drink that she needed. The damn chicken was lodged in her throat. She waved her arms frantically.

"Mom, what's wrong with Auntie Kate?"

Liz looked up from Ned, who'd begun tugging on the buttons of her blouse. "Kate?" In a flash, their eyes met, and Liz pushed her chair back, yelling for help and someone to take Ned out of her arms. Kate was thinking Liz could do anything, including handing off her youngest child, leaping over a fallen chair, and performing a perfect Heimlich maneuver.

Yeah, I can't breathe but hoo boy, I'm thinking a cheer.

A pair of arms wrapped around her upper belly at the bra line, ripping her from the chair, which clattered to the linoleum floor. In slow motion, she saw Jake Jr.'s eyes filling with tears. There was the grip of someone punching her gut. She tried to focus, but things went black.

***

Caleb had wanted to change out of his costume, but despite the sign indicating Santa needed a break, finishing off the line of kids and parents took too much time. At the risk of being mobbed in his Santa suit, he rushed to the mezzanine, trusting kids and parents alike wouldn't molest him when he tried to grab a bite. As much as he'd like to sit and enjoy the company of Liz, the children, and the bookish girl, it might not be possible. He figured if he showed up as Santa in the café, the worst that might happen was a few excited children would get an extra ho-ho-ho, and then he could stop for a few minutes at the Willis table to enjoy a few minutes more of Kate O'Malley.

Besides, being out of costume meant running a risk that Jake Jr. might see through Cal without the costume, put two and two together, and realize Santa in uniform and Cal in street clothes were the same person. He didn't need to worry about Sam because she'd joined forces with her mother to set up the meeting with Kate. As he ticked off all the pros and cons in his head, Cal accepted first and foremost that he didn't want to ruin Christmas for the Willis children. He tried to soften his Texas accent when he played Santa, but Ms. Nanny-Editor, Kate O'Malley, fired him up somehow, and he'd lost focus, settling into himself despite the costume.

It wasn't that he was ashamed of his roots. More importantly, he refused to be embarrassed by owning a cattle ranch. Tofu folks could protest all they wanted. Caleb Walker raised prime beef for the restaurant market. He loved a great rare steak, seared with grill marks on the outside, and red, not pink, on the inside. He didn't mind the protests. Hell, Cal was all for free speech and no-holds-barred personal preferences for everybody. It all worked for him. The only time Cal got irritated was if a veggie-burger-loving, hemp-shirted hippie type jumped the fence, thinking a bull needed saving. The one time that had happened was almost tragic. Luckily, the nincompoop with the not-so-genius idea that his mission was to free a fourteen-hundred-pound animal with a five-foot horn spread hadn't been hurt. Equal rights were all fine and dandy, except where trespassing was the means to exercise a contrary opinion.

And Cal had reasons for keeping his natural style of speech at bay when he was playacting at Santa. He figured small children who still believed needed a neutral Claus. It might be silly, but he could imagine some city kid worrying because he didn't think they spoke Texas at the North Pole. Maybe he was set in his cowboy ways with no imagination. And in his head, he knew he was unfair because all the children he'd seen as "Santa" in the last two weeks had been okay.

He asked himself often enough when he was leaving for New York City why he'd agreed to Liz Willis's idea that he should live in New York for a while. Get a feel for everything, she'd said, and oh, by the way, why not take a part-time job as the Macho-Elf? Face it. Santa Claus was an elf. A drive-a-miniature-sleigh-with-tiny-reindeer, instead of a couple of broken broncs, elf. Caleb Walker? He was a cowboy.

There were many other reasons, some of which he might have mulled over if he hadn't spied Liz jumping out of her chair and heard Jake Jr.'s wailing. He could see Kate O'Malley's back with her hands at her throat, and Liz had started yelling for someone to call 9-1-1. Then quick-thinking Sam, standing on her chair with a rolled up paper menu fashioned as a megaphone, yelled out, "Is there a doctor in the house?"

If the situation weren't so serious, Cal would have burst out laughing. He'd seen a lot of people choke on beef, not so odd when one considered how many steakhouse meals he'd taken in over the years, but it was no longer a presumption that his maybe-editor had something lodged in her throat. It could be a cucumber for all he knew.

Crossing the distance in a matter of seconds, he reached under her breasts at the edge of her rib cage and simultaneously lurched her out of the chair while squeezing with a single pump under her ribs. If whatever was stuck in her windpipe didn't pop out, he'd have to take more drastic measures.

"Ewwwwww." Jake Jr.'s expression of childhood yuck said it all. Whatever had been choking Kate had flown across the table.

Sure enough, Sam held up a piece of something. "You got it, Santa. You got it. It's a big old piece of ABC chicken."

He wished he had time to enjoy Sam, but Kate was still limp in Cal's arms, her coloring hadn't returned to normal, and it seemed she wasn't breathing. He laid her flat on the cafeteria floor, ignoring the growing crowd of onlookers hovering like ghouls. Pinching her nose, tilting her neck gently, he breathed into her lungs. Shock waves raced along his mouth and down his jaw. Her lips were soft, full, and even half-blue, she was beautiful. It could be the lack of oxygen as everything about her had softened from harsh to serene, from anxious, to vulnerable.

The woman in his arms moaned softly.

"You're okay, Kate."

"Santa?"

"Front and center, ma'am."

"Don't," she coughed, and took a few short breaths, "call me ma'am."

"You're not in a position to give me orders, Kate."

Her eyes widened. "Dammit." She fought Cal to remove his hold on her, with the stupid intent to stand up as if nothing had happened.

"Don't struggle." He'd gone from his knees to sitting next to Kate with her head in the apex of his crossed ankles. "You need to relax for a few minutes and breathe. Just breathe, Kate. I'm not going to bite."

"Humph." She tried to wiggle free, but Cal held her still. His forearms curled beneath her armpits, which was how he would have helped her up, given half a chance. But the once-serene choking victim slipped his grip and, now on her knees, was preparing to shove off the floor when the cavalry arrived.

"Out of the way, excuse us, let us through." The paramedic team was working its way through the cafeteria-goers.

"Oh no, you don't." Kate leaned back farther on her haunches as if prepared to launch herself like a jungle cat from chair to chair to the elevator. She might have, but no kidding, like a danged Christmas miracle, Jake Jr. accidentally knocked over a full glass of milk. It spread across the table like some paper towel commercial and spilled off the edge to drip down Kate's back.

"Are you effing kidding me?" All propriety he'd previously seen in his assigned editor left as if by exorcism. She jumped up, grabbed her purse, and bolted past the EMTs even as one tried to grab her arm.

"Oh dear." For a moment, Liz appeared stunned but then turned to a white-haired older woman who'd taken Ned off her hands when Kate was choking. "Thanks for your help." She searched the crowd, as did Cal. The errant editor had her back to the cafeteria and shifted back and forth from one foot to the other as if that would make the elevator in a crowded department store two weeks before Christmas get to the mezzanine level any sooner.

"I guess we won't get that lunch, Mrs. Willis." He winked, the idea of him going to Kate's rescue absurd, but it had to be—red suit, white beard, black boots, and all.

"Thanks, Ca— Santa."

"Mom, Santa's going to save Auntie Kate, right?"

Uncertain why Jake Jr. had taken to calling the editor Auntie was a question that had to wait because for now, three anxious EMTs were putting on a full blitz toward Kate. Santa or not, Cal intended to get there first.

It didn't take all of thirty seconds, but when he arrived, Kate had shoved an EMT away. "I'm fine." She spotted Cal over the shoulder of the first responder. "Ask Santa. He's right behind you."

"Ms. O'Malley, we want to take your blood pressure and check your throat. Also, we need to see if you broke anything, or there's bruising around your ribs. You were given CPR—"

"By jolly old freakin' Mr. Claus there." Kate pointed an index finger over the medic's shoulder. "And rest assured, I'm quite aware I received CPR. I no doubt have the bruises as proof."

"That's our point, ma'am, but it doesn't matter who administered the life-saving procedure, which it probably was in your case. Bottom line, we were dispatched, and it will help us out if you'd calm down and let us take a few notes. Then you can go, and we'll be on our way to help someone who needs it."

No sarcasm in that comment and it made Cal smile. He was surprised Kate didn't protest the title of "ma'am." Kate's reaction to the EMTs made Cal feel better about how she behaved around him. Of course, he'd pushed some buttons on purpose during their subway exchange, but she did something to him, something he hadn't felt in ten years. The first time he'd seen her hunkered down in her cubby at the publishing office, electric-like sensations had raced up and down his nerves from his brain to every distant point in his body. He should have been introduced then, but some other editor, Matt something, had pulled him into an office to discuss the possible book contract.

"Ms. O'Malley will cooperate with you good people." He grinned at Kate over the head of the NYC Fire Department paramedic. "Won't you, ma'am?"

"I will not."

"Ah, touchy, stubborn, and stupid."

"I am *not* stupid."

"Good, then we have an admission to touchy and stubborn?"

"You, Santa, are an ass."

"Maybe, but I don't intend my efforts at saving you to end up on the wrong end of a lawsuit, so if you don't mind, let these nice folks check you out and confirm my CPR neither broke anything nor ruined your ability to edit my book."

"Hey, Santa, you wrote a book? Cool." This from the one female on the rescue team. "Is it, you know, literature, or spicy?"

"It's romance, so I'm not sure where you'd put it on a shelf, but it's rated X."

"Yikes." The short, slightly plump, but muscular EMT smiled, her blues eyes sparkling against pale cheeks. "Well, we won't blow your cover here, Santa. Maybe when it's published?" She smiled again, this time taking Kate's left arm and gently ushering her to a manager's office to the left of the elevator. "When you get published," she stopped and reached into her shirt pocket, beneath a badge that said "EMT, S. Fisher, #23"—Cal didn't get all the numbers, "here's my card. You could autograph a copy and send it over. I promise I'll share your book with as many folks as I can."

"I'll make sure you get a copy, Officer Fisher. It won't be out until next Christmas though."

"No biggie, time flies in this job." She had Kate on a chair tucked in the corner of the office, away from prying eyes. Cal followed, leaning against the door frame, further blocking the curious crowd from any view of Kate and watching the process of the medical tech's examination. Lying to himself, he let his brain believe this was solely to protect his interests. As the EMT removed Kate's jacket, he noted that the blouse needed to be unbuttoned because of its tailored touches, recognizing the pleats pinched the shirt to form fit beneath her breasts. A slim green belt held the plaid skirt in place, the shirttail even now being tugged at by the paramedic.

"Sir, could we get a little privacy for Ms. O'Malley, right? O'Malley?"

A terse, "Yes," was Kate's only reply.

"Oh, sure." Cal turned his back, although he had been enjoying the mechanical unpacking of Ms. Priss from her wrapping. "But I'm staying until you give her a clean bill of health, at least as far as this incident and the CPR goes."

"Sure, Santa."

"Double-ass." Kate's tone expressed anger. At least she wasn't taking it out on the EMT team anymore. "That's tight, ow." She must be referencing the blood pressure cuff.

Cal took the time of Ms. O'Malley's examination to revisit how he'd ended up in this predicament. It was about the book. They said the world revolved around story, but he couldn't write anything as good as the last few minutes. Too bad he had to get back to his Santa duties, and he hadn't had lunch, so he shoved two dollars into a vending machine and reached for some candy bar with at least the nutritional value of peanuts.

That first day, the day he'd seen a passing glance of his would-be editor, Jake Willis had informed Cal in a straightforward way that the book was only being considered at his wife's request, and that she'd chosen Kate O'Malley to review and edit the manuscript. Liz Willis had somehow managed to write a great Christmas book three of the last five years, and Cal didn't doubt her ability to be right about his work. He made a promise to himself not to distrust her suggestions. Besides, how could he complain about being introduced to a co-founder of Bennett & Willis?

That any one editor over another should edit Cal's book was not only out of his control, but of little consequence. Or so he'd thought. And then he'd heard, rumor only, that the editor assigned was a square, a stick-in-the-mud for traditional, contemporary romance. It seemed possible that O'Malley could kick his work to the curb on archaic principles. And that's why he'd accidentally on purpose run into Kate on the subway.

Still, Liz loved the book. She said she had a few "niggles," or what she called her suggestions, but otherwise, she was on his side. He'd read her books and remained envious of her ability to tell a story with characters in ashes. She was able to raise two souls from horrific loss to find love again, to move on.

Not something Cal had been able to do, but he'd taken a turn at writing a romance, in part at the suggestion of his oldest friend. Plus, the genre had changed a lot in twenty years, and there was room for a silver-belt-buckle-wearing, sometimes-bitter cowboy to submit a so-called romance. Of course, from his perspective, any good book started with hot sex around page—well, page one.

He returned his thoughts to the girl being tended to by the EMTs. Slip and bra, or only a bra? Cal stared straight at the elevator arrow across the hall, but it was killing him not to turn around and satisfy his curiosity. Simple or lacy? He bet ten dollars that her undergarments were anything but fancy.

"Hey, Santa. Behind you. We're all done."

Cal turned. Towering over the female EMT, he could see over her head, taking in the woman he'd saved. She was standing, buttoning up her shirt, shoving the tail of the crisp white cotton beneath the belt. The office was too warm, at least to Cal in his Santa suit.

His watch buzzed against a wrist. Damn, he was ten minutes over his "Santa's Shop Opens Again at 1 p.m." deadline. Hell, he didn't need the job. He'd taken it to figure out how little kids thought because he was entertaining the thought of writing a young adult series, opposite extremes to the current book. Cal figured if he went through with it, he'd use a pseudonym. He had a main character in his head, a troubled babysitter modeled after a girl he'd known so long ago, a friend from foster care. Cal hoped working on the story would have a liberating effect, might even help erase the nightmares. Staring at his maybe-editor, Cal was tempted to blow off going back to Santa-land. Maybe she'd like him if he stuck to writing kids' books or teen fiction.

"Santa, you did fine. No busted ribs, a little tenderness, no permanent damage to her windpipe. We think the blackened chicken might have caused a separate reaction, an allergy? She's been told to check that out."

"Sheila, let's go, we got another call."

"Right, well, thanks, and don't lose that card, Mr. Claus."

"I wouldn't dream of it."

The team turned sideways to Cal, who edged farther into the office to let them by. They then dashed toward the emergency exit. There seemed no reason for them to wait for an elevator or brave a crowded escalator, and all three looked in great shape. He imagined they ate staircases for breakfast, so he turned to face Kate.

"Get out of my way, you big red fake."

"Kate, it's not my fault I—"

"You've somehow insinuated yourself into my life. I don't know whether Liz or Jake, hell, or both are behind it, but I'm not interested." She shoved past him and stormed toward the same emergency exit taken by the rescue team. After a pause, she settled on the elevator and punched the button like it was a bad guy. He stared at her ponytail, thinking it would be a wonderful way to tug her head back and nibble on her neck gently.

But then she turned, her eyes like lasers, grilling Cal like the steaks he loved. Straightening her shoulders, she shoved an uncooperative purse back up her left arm. "I'm going to let Jake Willis know I wouldn't read your book now for pleasure, let alone editing, even if I get fired for it."

He stared as the elevator opened. Kate crammed her way into a full car, and then the doors closed on her steely gaze. Even if Kate read his book, the likelihood that she'd ever let him hold her, kiss her, damn, take her to bed, vanished as she had behind the elevator doors.

"Well, CJ, you blew that." Oh, he knew it, but saying it aloud to nobody, in particular, helped Cal process the last few hours. And how the hell did she get under his skin so quickly?

And since she had, now what?

Chapter 8

Jake Sr. looked down at his wife. Liz Willis to the world, Lizzie Callahan to him, always and forever. He would never tire of loving her, of being loved by her, of holding, touching, listening to her breathe. Of course, these days, the added sound of a baby monitor in the nursery was always attendant—in truth, it had been for the last six years. There was still a concern that the curious minds, watchful eyes, and attentive ears of Sam, Jake Jr., and now Eric 2 might be a problem when Jake and Liz made love. He chuckled to himself because now they had to remember to lock the door.

He looked around the room as he ran fingers through the tangled mat of Lizzie's hair spread across his chest. Thank God for LED candles. Lizzie's practice of putting candles everywhere when they made love had been squelched, but she wouldn't give up the incense. So the building wouldn't burn down, but the room still smelled like a '70s headshop. Liz swore incense helped get her into "super-hot mode," so he'd learned to appreciate the strong scents of patchouli, jasmine, and one that sounded like bathroom cleaner, forest something? Jake had no intention of messing with Lizzie's science— not unless he stopped breathing.

Now, studying the top of Lizzie's head, he was a little worried about his wife's determination to make a match between his editor, Kate O'Malley, and a potential new writer to the house, Caleb Walker. Especially since the editor in question seemed so out of sorts with men, and the book was beyond a bodice ripper, its author a larger-than-life cowboy. Jake had doubts about venturing into explicit sex as a line, but Bennett & Willis had partners now, and he'd given up some control on purpose.

His doubts extended to Kate's ability to edit a book that spontaneously burst into flames in the first few pages. That kind of sexuality struck Jake as way out of Kate's league.

"Hey, you." Lizzie stirred and laid her chin on his chest. "Your brow is furrowed. Not fair after that super-hot encounter. Your face should be melting into the pillow, Mr. Willis."

Jake chuckled and pulled her up to his chest. "It melted, but I had it reconstituted with help from our shape-shifters romance department."

She flicked a thumb against his nipple. "Brat."

"Goddess."

"Oh, that's so cheating, Jake Willis. You know I languish when you treat me to the compliments I so richly deserve." She laughed and lifted the sheet to look at his groin. "Maybe, if you entice me enough with flattery, I'll do something extra for my man."

"Lord, Lizzie, I'm done, you know I'm pushing old age here."

She straddled his chest. "So not."

"Am."

"Am not."

"Sentence fragment, wife."

"You know what Jake Jr. told Santa today, Mr. Willis?"

"Not sure. You regaled me with the nightmare in the cafeteria, but I've heard nothing about the visit to our scintillating romance-writing Santa."

"He told Santa that 'absopositive' was a word, but 'absopositively' would be adverb abuse." She grinned like Seuss's Grinch. "If you recall, I once busted you on that grammatical faux pas."

"Other way around, Mrs. Willis. I red-circled multiple 'LY' words in your work, but I think we should campaign to get 'absopositive' into the dictionary."

"Hmmm, I don't remember your charges about my abuse of the trusty adverb quite the same way, publisher-man, but you're right about the word. It's great, right? I can't believe we have such clever children." She plucked a hair from Jake's head.

"Ow. Dammit, Liz."

"Oh, nonsense, you wuss. If you're going to worry about your dotage when you are still all man and all mine, I'm going to continue to keep the real gray at bay. Hah. That's funny. I'm a poet."

"You're a nutcase."

"So you say, Jake Willis, but that psychiatric diagnosis keeps you on your toes. You know damned well you'd perish were I normal."

"Ha, funny."

"Told ya that years ago."

"And never stop being that way." He brushed a frizzy lock of hair off her forehead and tipped her chin up so that she'd have to look at him without evasion. "Now, let's get back to the subject we were on before you distracted me with...you know...and," he used his index finger to survey the room, "one, two, three-four-five, six, and what...three on the dresser?" He licked his finger and stuck it in one of her ears. "Candle freak."

"Yech, Jake, a wet willy?"

"Hmmm, when you say it, sounds sexy instead of gross."

"Well..." One hand drifted down his belly, attempting to get under the covers.

"No distractions, missus."

"Okay then. Back to my plan. We have to do something, Jake. And besides, it affects the business."

He groaned. So far, Lizzie's plotting worked for the better, but the way she delivered that last "affects the business" bit sounded a tad ominous, even for his wife. "Liz..."

"Oh honey, you'll fix it. You're the boss." Her fingers tapped an unknown tune on his chest. Jake had always loved the finger music against his skin, but this time, he grabbed her hand and her attention. "Fix what?"

"Uh..." Liz looked away, and he had to pull her chin back to force her focus. "Cal told me after the whole EMT brouhaha that Kate kind of quit."

Jake tugged hard and sat up against the headboard with Lizzie in tow. "What?"

"Come on, Jake. She was royally embarrassed and pissed off about something Caleb, well, Santa did after practically saving her life, and..."

"And what?"

"Said she wouldn't read or edit Cal's book, even if it meant getting fired."

Jake loved Liz, and it still surprised him when he wanted to simultaneously strangle her and yet kiss the worried expression from her face. He had to think of his life before Lizzie to keep from flipping out when she did something to throw his world off-balance.

"We may lose an author, or an editor, depending on one's perspective. Especially if you insist on matchmaking between the Texas cowboy inclined toward a couple of hundred shades of gray in his writing, and the proper editor—one I think has immense potential but who will hightail it back to Nowhere North Dakota if you don't back off."

"Jake, you are such a liar. Katie's from California, not North Dakota, and besides, that's judgmental. I hear that the Dakotas aren't all bad. Maybe a little cold sometimes. Besides, your big bad partner act can't fool me. You don't want Kate to be alone any more than I do." She circled his abdomen lightly with her fingers. "And you know I'm right. You can't stop it if I'm right. They belong together."

"Lizzie, how can you be so effing sure?"

"Honestly, Jake. You don't see it?"

"No."

"Because, Mr. Willis, opposites attract. Or did you forget that?" Liz escaped his grasp, burying her head beneath the covers.

"Damn it, Lizzie, we need to..." There was nothing for it. "Sweet Jes—"

She popped her head up long enough to giggle. "No, cursing, Jake."

"Well, what would you have me..." but he could get no comprehensible sounds out. Jake gave up. Lizzie always won. With a moan, he let her.

Chapter 9

Kate had deserted social media, at least for the time being, and with good reason. The Department-Store-Santa-Saves-Woman-in-Cafeteria story had made Twitter. No identities of the players were available, but it was enough to see someone's cell phone video of Santa yanking an unidentified woman out of her chair. Instead of spending hours on her computer, she sat staring at her big-screen TV, the sound on mute. *Miracle on 34th Street*, memorized in her brain, she couldn't stand the goody-goody shit tonight, of all nights, but there wasn't much else on. "I believe, I believe, it's silly but I believe." All credit to the young actor, Natalie Wood. Suzy, right, that was her name in the movie. Kate had a dilemma of her own and spoke to the muted image on the screen. "I have got major Santa issues, Suzy. You've no idea."

Thirty-two years old, biological clock ticking away, loud enough to be Poe's *Tell-tale Heart*. Tick-tock, tick-tock. "Crap." And why did it matter? Was it ingrained in their society, that whole wife-and-mother thing? For Kate, it didn't matter anyway. As far as she was concerned that ship had not only sailed, it'd sunk.

"Today, world," she tipped her wineglass at the TV, "I completely eff'd up." Announcing that she'd quit rather than read Caleb Walker's book—dumb. She would appear less than competent and, to the big boss, as anything but an open-minded editor capable of editor-like stuff like finding or editing bestsellers.

Worse, it would now be apparent to anyone and everyone at Bennett & Willis that Ms. Editor O'Malley was, indeed, a prude. Frigid. Milk-toast. Well, if the pump fits. Kate was petrified of sex, whether on the pages of a book or spoken in her ear in a moonlit room, hands caressing her body, kisses on her neck. That she'd fooled around with Matt was not only a monumental mistake. She'd only pretended to enjoy it, but the truth, the sum of her sexual experiences totaled two.

Kate lost her virginity on New Year's Eve of her senior year. That she did it on purpose didn't help. She wanted the event done and over with, no strings attached, no whistles, bells, bows, no slippery, sexy, sliding off chairs onto the floor and shit—nothing like that.

And it hadn't been like that. Russ Martin, also a senior, was on the tennis team and ran track. Handsome? Nah, but he was on an Ivy League projectile, and he too had a mission. Get it done. She hadn't believed in happily ever after then, and she didn't now. No sense in trying to explain that to her boss.

She was a damned good editor, and that was all she wanted to be.

"Dammit, dammit, dammit." She jumped up from the sofa and nearly fell, having forgotten she was wearing her big blue Smurf slippers. Hey, who was she to reject the white elephant gift from last year's office party?

She righted herself, but not before banging her right shin on the coffee table. "Shit." Rubbing the instant bump, she eyed the bottle of Chardonnay. Only eight ounces were missing from the bottle. She'd measured her intake—two one-half cups poured into a Lalique wineglass. Her mother had left her china and crystal. The woman who gave her birth hadn't spoiled Kate. The downfall in parenting had been leaving an only child to her own devices from the age of eight, when her dad died, until, well, forever. Her mother, widowed, uneducated, and not much in the till to support herself, let alone a young daughter, had managed.

There were men. They had come in all shapes and sizes. The worst of them had fondled Kate. The best ignored her, and as a result, Kate's fantasy world had taken her to books. Anything but romance. Kate simply didn't believe in happy endings.

"Whoopee, I'm an editor. And rightly so, dammit." The fruits of her labor hadn't amounted to any change in her mother's lifestyle, but what heirlooms her mom had from her family, and what she saved, she'd left for Kate. No formula would create a family from the remnants of her mom. Except that upon her mother's death, Kate learned of the trust fund. So, Kate had money, expensive crystal, sterling silver, and fine bone china.

Maybe if Kate ever felt comfortable entertaining anyone, including men, she'd whip out the collection to a bunch of oohs and ahs. A stab of guilt struck because it wasn't fair to think ill of her mom. She'd been somewhat of a success in the film industry. At the thought, Kate snorted wine out through her nose. "Gross." Wiping her nose with the back of her sleeve, she experienced a moment of self-loathing that she even relied on the trust. Kate shuddered at the origin of her annuity, trying to keep the spirit of the season in her heart, trying to hold the demons at bay.

"And what are you going to do about being fired, O'Malley?" *Am I fired? Entirely possible.* Officially rejecting the author brought into the house by Jake Willis's legendary wife had been stupid. "I'd give anything to be like you, Lizzie." Kate raised her glass to the ceiling. Then pouring without measuring, she headed for the kitchen. Food would be good, something she knew even as she slugged more of the very dry but extremely tasty Napa-Sonoma wine.

***

Cal stared up at the renovated brownstone. He'd done his reconnaisance, noting there were four separate apartments in the building. Katie was on the second floor, left side of the building facing him as he stood in the shadows across the street. She must be doing well as an editor because Tribeca wasn't cheap.

The glow of the TV suddenly lessened as a light came on. Given the pendant-style lamps hanging from the ceiling, he had to assume that Ms. O'Malley was in the kitchen. His desire for her was so wrong and yet so compelling he needed to believe it was right.

After this afternoon, he didn't care if she wouldn't read his book. Not entirely true, but he felt a need to show her what it felt like to be wrong. He'd met her twice officially, both events resulting in her being moody, pissed off, and disinterested. So how come he felt as though it was inevitable for them to be together?

Maybe he should blame that on Liz Willis. The woman seemed hell-bent on match-making them together. Editor and writer? He guessed she got the idea from her own life. Still, the planned lunch had been a disaster. Kate standing in line with the kids to see Santa—also a complete nightmare. It sure as hell didn't endear Kate to Cal as a writer or a person.

It was mostly dumb to stalk the woman from outside, in the cold, when he'd planned to seduce her, sweep her off her feet. "That's some romantic crap, CJ." It wasn't a question of sex, not at all. Cal felt something weird and inexplicable in terms of an emotional reaction to the girl. And what was he going to do about it? He had to do something quickly. It was dipping below 30 degrees tonight.

Fastening a few buttons on his jacket, he took a deep breath and crossed the quiet street to the four mailboxes with buzzers outside the entrance. He took a chance on three and pushed the button, figuring he'd nothing to lose, except getting his novel published.

Silence. He counted off twenty seconds. "Hello?"

He fist-punched the air. He'd chosen well. "Kate?"

"I didn't order anything, although I wish I had. Do you have pizza?"

He wished he did. "No."

"Who is this?"

"Caleb Walker."

"Freakin' Santa?"

"Could you please get past the Santa thing?"

"What if I want something for Christmas?"

He should leave, as it was obvious she'd been drinking. "How much have you had to drink, Kate?"

"Like that's your business."

"I'd like to make you my business, Kate."

Silence.

"Kate?"

"Yeah?"

"You okay?"

"Hell no." She sounded tearful.

"Please, let me help."

"You know how you can help me, cowboy?"

At least she left off the Santa bit. "How?"

"I need food. Come back with a pizza, pronto."

"Where would I get pizza at 8:20 at night?"

"Geeze, Santa-boy, this is New York City. You know, the city that never sleeps, all that garbage?"

"Nope. I live on a ranch."

"You're a hoot."

"Now you sound like me. But where, Katie, where should I get pizza that's fast and satisfactory?"

"That sounds like the first page of your book, cowpoke."

"Damn you, Kate. I'm trying to help." But her comment meant she'd at least read a few pages.

Kate hiccupped. "Oh, right. Sorry. Sausage and olive. Get large, and then if you're hungry, you can have a slice without stealing mine. And breadsticks and blue cheese dressing."

His stomach flipped at the order. "Where?"

"Two blocks down, all night take and bake. I'll turn the oven on. Peace out."

She'd hung up. Two blocks in which direction? Funny, Cal never got lost on over five thousand acres of ranch. Two blocks here was like being on Mars. Although it was December and cold, there was no snow in the forecast, at least until tomorrow. So, under what might be a starlit sky—which he couldn't tell because it was bright New York City that never slept, etc.—he took a chance on heading toward storefronts he'd seen from the cab, a few blocks back.

***

He wouldn't come back, but Kate put a bottle of red in the fridge to chill. *Yes, people, red is okay chilled.* At least in her book. Why she took two clean wineglasses out of the cupboard, Kate wasn't sure, but she tucked the bottle of Chardonnay in the back of the refrigerator and carefully washed the crystal glass.

Looking down at her Smurf slippers, Kate queried, "Do you think Santa Cowboy will mind the cheap wineglasses, guys?" Hearing herself aloud made Kate wonder if it should be Cowboy Santa instead of the other way around. "Oh well." She pondered the slippers a few seconds more, then, "Shit. I need to pee before he comes back. And brush my teeth." These important things she could do, even when tipsy, but Kate would be hog-tied, which was funny given the cowboy was a rancher, if she were going to change into something sexy.

She looked in the hall mirror. "I'm cute, right?" Unlike Snow White's mirror, the antique in the entryway didn't pass judgment. Of course, Kate usually took care of that without help from anyone else.

Spinning on the tile, she almost fell on her butt, yet managed to get to the bathroom and take care of immediate necessities. She skipped on the toothbrush, opting instead for a big gulp of blue mouthwash. "Like my Smurf slippers. Hah."

The buzzer blared from below.

***

Silence. *How long before I should buzz again?* Cal held a plastic-wrapped pizza on flimsy cardboard. It was heavy because on a hunch he'd paid for extra sausage and olive. The breadsticks also required baking in the oven. He only hoped that Kate had remembered to turn hers on as promised because she needed to eat, and his stomach growled. What if there was a pilot light and it had gone out?

He counted ten and hit the buzzer. The place hadn't exploded yet. Still, he should get upstairs and see if his hero skills were needed again. His might-be editor wasn't a complete flake, but it worried him since it was evident she'd hit the sauce a bit before he showed up a while ago.

"That you, pizza man?"

At least she'd stopped the Santa-Cowboy bit. "Yes, ma'am."

"You can't come up unless you promise not to call me ma'am."

"Okay."

"Okay, what?"

"Okay." A deep breath, "Okay, I promise."

"Better. My place is up the stairs on the left." The bell rang, and the door bolt clicked. There was no elevator, remodeled or not. The place would have lost too much square footage for a lift. With apartment doors on either side of the foyer, he trudged up to the second floor. His hand was up to knock when the door flew open.

"I'm starved, but I'm not going to give you that bit about being a lifesaver. I have toast and peanut butter, but pizza is so much better, right?"

"I like steak."

"Did you bring steak? I love steak."

"So why order pizza?"

"Well, you're some kind of cowboy, and I didn't want you going all Trivial Pursuit on me and explaining, like, the parts of a cow and stuff. Plus that would have been a pretty complicated order."

Cal's head was spinning a little, and he was stone-cold sober. He held out the cardboard covered take-and-bake pizza, the breadsticks, and, not wanting to have the door slammed in his face, he kept back the blue cheese dressing packed in a tin container with a cardboard lid. He figured it a valuable enough commodity to work as ransom.

"Okay, thanks. Come in, I guess."

"You guess?"

"On one condition. I need to eat, and I don't want to talk about your book."

"That's two conditions."

"Okay, well, did I make both conditions clear enough for you, smart-ass?"

"Indeed." He stepped into the small entryway of the apartment, closing the door behind him. The click sounded secure, but he wondered about the chain and two deadbolts. "You feel safe here, do you?"

"I do. But I'm not stupid." She leaned past him, brushing his coat with her arm, and slammed the two bolts across the door. "The chain is useless, might as well be an ankle bracelet, but the bolts, those babies are solid."

Cal watched her head to the kitchen, a bit stunned by Kate's quirky alter ego. He chalked it up to an anomaly and, no doubt, to alcohol.

The apartment had been redone so that kitchen, dining, and living room were one large open space. A bar ran the length of the kitchen sink, surrounded by a butcher block. A dish drainer sat in one half of the sink, a larger basin with two compartments in the other. A separated small circle with a drain sat high up in the sink, containing a garbage disposal. "I don't know much about New York City, but how'd you swing this place on an editor's salary?"

"You mean if I don't mind your nosing into my business?"

"Well, I'm here for a bit, and I did a little research because it would be stupid not to. At least that's my perspective."

"Okay, that makes sense but it's still none of your business."

"Probably not."

"You've created the elephant in the room, you know, and made me uncomfortable." Kate put the pizza down to the left of the sink, and with a knife from a block, she sliced through the plastic seal. She had a pizza-spatula thing, whatever it was called, and she turned, slipping the pie onto a shelf of the built-in oven, winding a timer with a flourish. The apparatus was Bugs Bunny's head, with the numbers for minutes around the base. Cal shifted his gaze to the TV, wondering if Looney Tunes was on. He was partial to the buzzard cartoon, the one where the bird was bringing home a baby bumblebee. His chuckle didn't escape her.

"What's so funny?"

"It's complicated. But you've got *Miracle on 34th Street* on. A story every writer wishes

they'd written." He didn't say that the part of Maureen O'Hara reminded him of the editor persona of the girl now baking a pizza in some kind of pajama getup. *Pretty damned ironic.*

She quirked her head sideways, which made the ponytail bob. "Do you wish you'd written it? I mean, without the smut?"

"Unfair, Kate. You haven't read my book."

"Yeah. I'm sorry."

Cal decided against harassing her about the comment, at least for now. "What about the breadsticks?"

"Oh, too soon, they barely need to be baked, best all gooey and dipped in the blue cheese. Where is it? Did you remember?"

Cal handed her the bag.

"Oh, I don't like you much, cowboy, but you can follow directions. That's a good sign." She opened the dressing and dipped a finger in, raised it to her mouth, and licked.

His desire for her was in overdrive as it was. Cal didn't need her licking another drop off her finger, so he snatched the container from her hand. "Looks like an amazing taste sensation but what say we save it for the breadsticks?"

She cast him a sideways glance. "Okay, if you insist. Have you tried it before?"

"Would that I could have, Ms. O'Malley."

"Okay, well, that made no sense to me. Want a glass of red?"

He spied the two clean glasses on the countertop next to the fridge. "Sure. When in Rome…"

"Right, except this is New York and it's early. We should go dancing."

"Huh?" Kate was a non sequitur on long legs.

"I'm kidding. Shoot, your coat and hat."

"I like 'em without holes, ma'am."

"That was an expression, and you damned well know it." She put her hand out. "You must want to lose your coat? The hat can stay if you promise not to do that cowboy hat-tipping thing."

"Uh, yes. I don't need the hat, unless you have a hot Texas sun and a couple of hundred head of cattle around. Thanks." *And you can take my shirt, my pants, shoes, socks. All of it, Ms. O'Malley, I'd take it all off for you.* Cal shrugged out of the thick navy overcoat, handing it to Kate. Their hands brushed, she blushed, and a certain part of his anatomy stirred. Laying the coat over the back of the couch, she hooked his hat on the ladder back of a dining chair and returned to her kitchen.

Cal walked around the area. There was a modest oak dining table with four chairs, the large, overstuffed sofa holding his coat, and a matching chair that sat at an angle to the couch under a reading lamp. Windows to the street didn't reveal much of a view, but it was a nice street. The cushioned built-in seat would make for a good place to while away a rainy day reading a book—his book.

"The bath is through that door at the end of the hall. It's to the right when you enter the bedroom."

"Good to know." He grinned at her, enjoying the sudden flush in her cheeks. She blushed beautifully. And it only took the word "bedroom" to get her reaction.

"Well," she ducked her head to avoid looking him straight on, "I mean, I didn't want you to think I lived in a wooden shoe or something."

"It's roomy, well designed, and seems like a nice neighborhood." He smiled. "Of course, I know nothing about New York."

She'd poured the wine and walked toward him, and it seemed to Cal like she was scared. "You entertain much, Kate?"

"No, not much. I almost live at the office."

"So I've heard."

"We're not talking about the book, remember?"

"I remember." The pizza timer dinged, and Kate turned away without handing him the wineglass. With an oven mitt covering one hand and the spatula-thing in the other, she resembled an exterminator as she removed the pie without incident, slipping it, lightly browned edges and all, onto the cutting board.

"That needs to cool. So, in go the breadsticks." She twisted Bugs Bunny again, but brought it back to a few minutes, setting it on the counter. Reaching above her head, she pulled two plates from a glass-doored cupboard and set them next to the pizza. The overhead stretch allowed him a glimpse of the purplish haze reflective of an injury.

"I'm sorry about the bruising, Kate. It happens with CPR."

"Right, you saved me today. Thanks."

He wouldn't push her. "We're eating pizza off china?"

"My mom's. I inherited it, along with some crystal and silver." She seemed distracted and reluctant to share how she came into money.

"You in there, Kate?"

"Sorry. So, you want to eat pizza with a silver fork or is stainless okay? Me? I'll eat the pie holding a slice in my hands."

"Oh, I think stainless. I don't want you to spend tomorrow polishing the silver, after all, you probably gave the staff Sunday off, right?"

"Cowboy, you have a weird sense of humor."

"At least I have one."

"Hey, that was a crummy thing to say."

"I know, I'm sorry, trying to get your goat a little I guess."

"Hmm. Well, knock it off." She'd seemed to remember something, and with a grin, Kate handed him the glass of wine. "I think you should sit right there at the bar. That way I can eat my pizza standing up. It burns more calories. Plus you don't get to look at my profile while I'm snarfing down a piece of pie."

"You have a nice profile, Ms. O'Malley."

"I don't, and there's no sense in pretending about it." She spun and tugged the breadsticks from the oven, placing them on a plate, then faced him on the other side of the counter. Cal thought wryly it was her armor—a tile and butcher block shield. With precision, she rolled a pizza cutter through the pie and carefully placed two slices on a plate, along with a fork, on the bar top in front of him.

She held up an index finger. "Wait for it..." then heaped a tablespoon of blue cheese dressing to the left of his two slices. "That stuff on a garlic breadstick is nirvana."

He wasn't sure that bread dipped in thick white dressing equated to bliss, but he was sure the girl was a slice of heaven. Screw the pie.

"Oops, hang on." Reaching into a deep second drawer, she yanked out two red cloth napkins. "Ta-da." The woman was, in short, delightful, despite the defense mechanisms used to keep people at bay. Flannel pajama pants were tied comfortably at the waist, while a bodysuit of some kind held her in beneath a waffled thermal tee. It didn't hide her nipples though. He continued his study, noting that her pants were plaid, like the skirt worn earlier that day, the shirt red.

His pizza chef was some kind of hot hippie-elf-nymph.

Cal wanted her, not the pizza. She was a smart, sexy woman, and the green eyes that smiled as she took her first bite of pizza made him weak at the knees.

"Eat or leave, cowboy."

"Guess the fork's unnecessary." Cal took a bite. If he ate slowly, if they could work their way through all the breadsticks, every slice of pizza, the dressing, and hopefully the wine, then maybe she'd let down her guard. Then, perhaps he could kiss her—long, sweetly, then hard, then all over.

"Hey, Santa, you daydreaming?" She winked. "Not about me, I hope. Not worth it."

"Maybe a little. You got to admit that Dior knockoff you have on will drive any man wild."

"Hah. That's way funny, but it's not likely I drive men crazy."

He let any further comment go. He ripped another bite of pie with his teeth. "Pretty damn good."

"I didn't think you beef-eatin' cowpokes had much experience with pizza."

"Steak strips on a fresh tortilla, wrapped up with cheese, olives, and killer pepper sauce…not so different. Like I said though, this," he held up the slice, "is good."

"No, *great*. Remember, I baked that sucker."

"Right."

She picked up one of his breadsticks and dragged it through the dressing. "Here." Reaching across the bar from her side of the sink, Kate put the dripping stick to his lips. Either he'd have to deal with a blob of dressing tumbling down his shirt, one that would no doubt stain, or bite. So he bit. Her grin was genuine and too damned sexy to describe. "Kind of like a rocket ship ride, right?" Matching dimples punched holes in her cheeks, and her damned ponytail bobbed again, back and forth behind her long, slender neck.

"No. It's not." Cal wasn't hungry. Not for food anyway. He slipped off his stool and rounded the bar in a heartbeat. He wanted to go to the moon on a rocket all right. "Maybe I don't get how to eat it. Maybe you should show me again."

Her eyes widened, and she tried to back away, but Cal stepped on the toe of one Smurf slipper, his left arm circled her and tugged. "I think you should demonstrate." He reached to her plate, dragged a breadstick through the dressing, and raised it to her mouth. "Show me, Katie."

If she were frightened, it didn't show in her face. But then again, Cal thought it might be her pride. That and the fact that she wouldn't give in, not like a woman full of desire. Nope, Kate was the kind of girl who had to keep control of her emotions. Something in her past, he suspected. Hell, he had the same problem.

She surprised him, biting the breadstick in his hand, and then licking her lips. "Satisfied, cowboy?"

"Not yet. No."

She stammered, then plowed forward. "It's not like I'm going to poison you to keep from reading your book."

"Nope. I didn't think so, but I'm thinking you need to realize that if you don't at least try to read it, I'll be mortally wounded."

"Geeze, Walker. Talk about being a drama queen."

"I'm reduced to begging, and you still won't concede to reading even a page or two?"

"I read more than fifteen pages already. I'm going to ask Jake to give it to another editor, it's not my style. I won't be of any help to you, so…"

He lifted her chin, a finger wiping the remnant of dressing away. "You're right about the blue cheese." He licked the drop from the end of his index finger. "It's stellar."

Kate gulped, tugging, trying to free herself from his grip. "You should go."

"I know." His finger dipped into the dressing on her plate again, and he deposited the tasty goo across her lower lip. "Would it surprise you that I don't want to leave?"

She didn't speak but shook her head left, right, left, right, then back to brave a candid look into his eyes. Cal relaxed his grip and stepped back. "I'm not taking you against your will, Katie."

"Kate."

"Katie. There is something inherently sweet about adding the 'i' and the 'e.' You can yell at me all you want, but since you refuse to read my book, it seems like we won't be working together, and you won't have to worry about me being around."

"You're so tall."

"Well, can't say as I ever heard that one before, ma'am. I mean, at least in terms of a rejection."

"It wasn't a rejection."

"Ah."

"No, not an 'ah' either. I can't do this. You *need* to go." There was a greater sense of urgency in her tone the second time.

"That's all I needed to hear tonight, Ms. O'Malley."

"What? That I can't...you know...I can't do this thing."

"No, that you weren't flat-out rejecting me. I get it. But 'can't' is not the same as 'won't.' Hope springs eternal."

"Dammit, don't quote stuff."

"Should I double my offense by suggesting that parting is such sweet sorrow?"

"I don't care who you quote. Pope, Shakespeare, it doesn't matter, it won't get you anywhere, cowboy."

"No? But I'm smitten." He bent and kissed her forehead. When she didn't move, he pressed his lips against her nose, then each corner of her mouth. "Totally smitten, Ms. Won't-Read-My-Book." At that, Cal rested his mouth against hers, and when she didn't object, he parted her lips with a kiss, his tongue flicking around hers...then he stepped back.

She stood, eyes closed, as if expecting more. God knew Cal wanted to give it to her. He wanted her and admitted to himself he had a deep need, one that went beyond the physical. Some empty part of his heart seemed filled when she was in the same room. He couldn't figure it out in a night though. That would need a lifetime.

"So, Madam Editor, I'll make you a deal."

"No way."

"Don't you think you should hear the offer first?" Cal forced himself not to lean back in and recapture the fresh soap scent of Kate. "I think it's reasonable."

"You would."

"Read eighty-five more pages. That puts you well into the story, the characters, you may even be able to guess at the end since it's, you know, happily ever after, as required by the genre."

"And then what?"

"If at a hundred pages you don't like it, I'll insist that Willis assign another editor and leave New York."

"What's the catch?"

"None, that's it. We'll call it our Christmas bargain."

"Oh, aren't you clever."

"I am. Do we have a deal?"

Kate looked down at her Smurf slippers. He still had the toe of one shoe holding her loosely captive at the edge of the bright blue slipper. She seemed to mull over the proposal, then raised her chin. "What happens if I can't stomach another eighty-five pages?"

"I stick around, drop by, bug you, that kind of thing."

"It feels like I lose both ways."

"You mean you'd miss me if I left?"

"Damn."

"In or out, Kate?"

"In." She almost smiled, and he saw a spark in her eyes that made it near impossible for Cal to keep his promise and leave.

"You are a most remarkable hostess, Ms. O'Malley. I'll see you tomorrow."

"Tomorrow? It's Sunday."

"Yes, ma'am. You going to church?" He studied her face, waiting to see if she'd make up a passion for religion to stay away from him. Nothing. "You need some sleep, and I'm not the kind of guy who takes advantage of a girl."

"Huh?"

Cal backed away, and the break in the connection he felt to Kate nearly submarined his resolve. Turning away, he grabbed his hat off the chair, his coat from the sofa back, stepped to the door, and slapped open the two deadbolts. "Promise you'll lock up behind me, sweetheart."

The sound of a pizza slice hitting the door gave him a sense of relief. She was pissed off enough to re-bolt the door and engage the flimsy security chain. Angry was good, although it meant one more obstacle he had to overcome, but he would.

Because damn if he wasn't falling in love with Kate O'Malley.

Chapter 10

Kate woke up in a fog, chased out of a dream she couldn't recall. It had seemed pleasant enough, but then again, so was her recollection of that kiss. "Damn, that jerk." He'd kissed her, and worse, she'd liked it. Kate had wanted more, but the crummy cowboy had deserted after two bites of pizza and a breadstick.

"That was some effing breadstick." Okay, in her head she knew she'd been swearing a lot lately. Even the faked "F" word was a negative thought. And it had all started when nimrod cowboy-Santa rode into town in his red suit. Correction—button-down jeans and a cowboy hat. "Who does that? Who still wears boots, and button-flies, and big freakin' rodeo hats?"

And who kissed her when she wanted to throw that very same person right out the second-story window? Kate tossed a pillow across the room. No damage was caused, but it did bounce off the mirror that ran the length of her closet. *Crud muffins*. Caleb Walker was hot. Too hot. Smart, clever, wicked funny, and hot. She jumped off the bed, and, because it felt right, stripped the sheets. It was her routine to clean house on Saturday, but the Willis-Santa debacle had interfered with the habit.

So, Sunday would have to do, and fresh linens would feel wonderful when she climbed into bed tonight. Alone.

There was no point in wasting a day fantasizing about a big, gorgeous cowboy hunk, so she put herself into housecleaning mode.

After starting a load of laundry in the stackable unit off the kitchen, she spray-waxed the snot out of all her furniture. Mr. Good-n-Clean something or other made the tile sparkle. She oiled the butcher block counter, cleaned the sink, grabbed a dying orange from the fridge, and sent a piece down the garbage disposal. After cleaning the bathroom, Kate surveyed the main living area. Magazines were neatly stacked on an end table, couch and chair cushions were plumped, and a sofa-throw was folded and hung over one arm at an angle appropriate for a photo shoot. She flicked the switch on the vacuum, her near-to-last chore. Kate ran the machine over the area rugs and under their edges, across the laminate floor, down the hall, and into the bedroom. She liked to get everything done at once, but the sheets were still in the dryer. Instead, she made sure any knickknacks, of which there were few, were arranged in a way that complemented her dresser.

Tempted to put the machine away, she took a deep breath and left it standing by the closet because inevitably, when she shook the sheets and bed cover, lint bunnies would appear from somewhere and float like some kind of annoying pixie dust onto the carpet.

Was it her fault she liked to see vacuum tracks across her carpets? Well, Kate didn't think so, but some people considered it a bit anal, more proof that she was uptight, OCD, whatever. The dryer buzzer sounded. Addressing the upright Hoover, she muttered, "Well, there you go," and turned to her last chore.

Fifteen minutes later, she could bounce a quarter off the bed and had wrestled the heavy rug sucker into the hall closet. Between the cleaners and polishes, the apartment smelled wonderful. Remembering the cowboy's question, Kate wondered why she didn't entertain. "Friends would help, Kate. Friends." Palming a threatened tear at the thought, she sat down at the dining table and stared at the manuscript. Shadows crossed the room, clouds no doubt, consistent with the weather report of rain and snow. She picked up Cal Walker's book and moved to the window seat. Outside, storefronts in mixed-use buildings reflected seasonal greetings and decorations.

"Kate, for a girl who loves Christmas, you sure know how to spend it alone." And that was sad. Her fake tree was in the basement, but she wasn't in the mood to pull it out. Maybe she'd get a live tree this year. She snorted. Probably a fat chance that'd happen.

She stopped staring into space and focused on the manuscript. Cal's novel. *The Christmas Bargain.* He'd thrown down the gauntlet, and so read it she would. It was too soon for wine, so she grabbed a diet soda from the fridge and plunked into her overstuffed chair with the book. The seat had long served as the antithesis of staying awake, and because of that quality, it was the perfect test of whether the cowboy's book was readable.

A pencil was tucked in where she'd left off yesterday at the office, so she didn't go back to the beginning. Hell, she remembered the beginning well enough to avoid rereading the sexually explicit introduction to the main characters. Walker's style put the book at somewhere between R and X-rated, and again she questioned her capabilities as its editor.

Am I a prude?

Kate shook off the idea and began to read.

***

Cal spent the morning talking with his ranch foreman, happy to find out there were no issues. Between Will Morgan—so much a cattleman he sometimes preferred the company of beef to ranch hands—Mrs. Withers—bookkeeper/housekeeper, kind-of-mom—and Cal's horse-crazy niece, Amanda, well, the place practically ran itself.

Sure, Will gave him grief about the novel, but Cal threatened him with the idea of making his oldest friend a character in his next book.

If this novel ever made it to print.

But no matter what he did, Cal's mind kept drifting back to his editor, and how to get her to read and like the book. Then he would find a way to charm her enough that she liked Cal. Not only hot stuff, like his writing, but the tender bit. The remedy for long-buried pain, for guilt, for anger that seeped through your skin.

And the kind of like that turned to love.

He wasn't sure Kate was the fix who'd calm the restlessness he'd felt for ten years, the thought of which reminded him of his ex. He wondered where Kelly was. He often did, although he long ago gave up caring if he ever saw her again. She was beautiful, brunette, and a cowgirl through and through. She'd been state champion in barrel racing several times, but that had never been enough.

The second time he'd caught her in the barn with a rodeo rider was the day he'd thrown her, and all her belongings, out. Worse, no belt buckles were involved. The man she left him for wasn't a rodeo rider but a wealth management guy. Hell, the divorce hadn't been a picnic, but that was the past, and he intended to leave it there.

Baggage? Yeah, he carried some. His weird foster care years could waylay Cal for hours if he'd nothing better to do. He kept busy and had finally seen someone to work through issues, but not for long. He only needed a jump start. The fact was the past had a way of digging into a body, and making it hard to break free.

But today, he had a commitment. He showered, shaved, figuring since the invite was indoors, it would be warm, so he donned a cotton shirt and a vest. Hmm, was that too cowboy? It didn't matter. He had to be himself. He could lose the vest if the Willises kept their apartment too warm.

Cal'd lost his parents and was separated from his only sister early in life, so family intrigued him. He longed for the chance to be a part of connected people, which meant he should be excited about the Sunday invite to his publisher's home. Still, he already understood that Liz Willis had a motive beyond the family getting to know Cal. The thought of her plan would have set off warning bells in the back of his mind, except Liz's plan involved a certain redheaded editor. And although rumors held a social meeting with Liz and Jake Willis was often a great benefit for a writer, the stories supporting Liz's crazy matchmaking schemes had basis in truth. Even though yesterday's infamous chicken adventure had curtailed the chance to get to know the kids, he worried that trying again so soon was risky. He hoped Liz had a plan to keep Jake Jr. from exclaiming that Cal was Santa.

In his head, Cal had every reason to believe that Liz Willis wasn't only going to make sure his book got published next year but, in the interim, that he found love. Not with just anyone, though. The connection planned by his boss's wife could only be with a certain prim editor at Bennett & Willis Publishing.

It turned out he now applauded the idea, but Cal had no intention of revealing his tête-à-tête with Kate O'Malley last night. He was happy knowing that she might not be as shy and retiring as everyone believed. On that thought, he grabbed his cell, the hotel room key, and went down to the lobby to catch a cab.

Chapter 11

Jake answered the door with his hand out. "Walker."

"Cal is appreciated, sir." They shook hands formally.

"Okay, but that means you toss the 'sir' bit."

"Done."

"It's Jake."

"Great."

"Come on in. Sam is holding court decorating the tree." This time, Jake patted Cal on the shoulder, nudging him out of the foyer and down two long steps to the brightly lit living room. A gas fire added to the homey feeling, as did the leather recliner, overstuffed sofa, and mahogany coffee table. There was a bar to the right, and behind that, a huge kitchen, big enough Cal couldn't see where it ended.

Tucking in his foot, Cal barely missed injury as Jake Jr. careened by on a tricycle. The middle Willis child spun in a circle and took off down an impossibly long hallway, singing "Jingle Bells."

"*He's* a happy kid," Cal murmured.

"Sorry about that." His boss stepped back up into the area that segued into the hallway and held up both hands like a police officer on a busy corner as he yelled, "Jake Willis Jr. Halt." The red three-wheeled pedal-operated vehicle slid to a stop at the edge of a built-in unit of shelves that appeared to run the length of the hall and was packed with books.

"Aw, Dad."

"Aw, Dad my-you-know-what. Park that thing and come back here. We have company, your mom is baking cookies, and you need to help Sam decorate the tree."

"Oh hey, the tree. Sorry, Dad." The meteor of a young boy dressed in cowboy boots, jeans, fake chaps, a fringed vest, and a holster with some kind of plastic gun raced back by without the wheels and pulled up to a dead stop as if he were riding the wildest bronc in the herd. "Howdy."

"Howdy, back." Cal smiled at Jake Jr. "Quite a rig you got there, cowpoke."

"Santa brought it last year. I don't get to wear it to school and stuff, but football's coming on. Mom says you like the team that's playing."

"I do. The Dallas Cowboys."

"They don't look like cowboys. Are you one, Mr. Walker?"

"I am."

Jake Jr. put out his hand so that Cal had to bend down a little to shake. "Mom taught us to shake hands."

"Good manners are one of the keys to success."

"Mom says that too, but she says school is especially important."

"Nice to meet you, Jake Jr."

"You sound like Santa. We saw him yesterday at the department store, and then he came to the lunch place and made a chicken come out of Aunt Kate's throat."

Damn. Cal swallowed. "Wow. But I can't be Santa. I'm a rancher from Texas. Santa sees a lot of kids in Texas, so maybe he picked up a little of our famous Texas twang."

"What's a twang?"

Cal's boss stepped in. "Son, Mr. Walker has a new book I'm trying to publish. He's visiting for the afternoon to watch the game. Also, your mom wants to speak with our guest about editing. I think one of Mom's important rules is not to pry."

"I forgot."

"It's okay, Jake, but the cookies are coming out of the oven one way or the other, and that tree won't get decorated by itself."

"Oh. Okay, Dad." The keen expression on Jake Jr.'s face said he didn't believe the man who came to watch a football game wasn't also Santa. He put out his hand for a second shake, and Cal wasn't sure it wasn't a test. The kid had spent quite a bit of time on Santa's lap yesterday morning.

Still, Cal completed the second shake. "Pleasure's mine." Comparisons between yesterday's Mr. Claus and the stranger in his living room hopefully diverted, Cal relaxed a bit when the younger Willis leapt over the back of the sofa to direct his sister on all things tree.

"Sam, you can't put the trolley car that low. Ned will try to eat it."

Sam waved. "Hi, Mr. Walker." She turned to her brother. "I can *so* put it there. Ned doesn't even like this dumb old souvenir. He'll try to eat the popcorn chains, though."

"It must be something, having all these kids, sir," Cal commented with a grin.

"Jake."

"I know, got it. But it sure seems like they add something to the holidays."

Before his boss could answer, Liz Willis skipped out of the kitchen with a tumbler and a plate of cookies. "Caleb Walker, of course they do. Children are equal parts annoying, challenging, but more than anything, a joy. I know you were married a long time ago. Any kids?"

"No. That relationship was pretty short-lived."

She offered him a cookie, which he dared not refuse, and then put the icy drink in his hands. "It's a weak mimosa, but Jake will mix you up something wicked if you want."

"Ah." Cal had been warned Liz was something of a tornado cut loose on a tumbleweed ranch. "Thanks. As to kids, my ex was more interested in winning and collecting national titles for barrel racing than having children."

"I'm sorry to hear that."

"Honest to gosh, Mr. Walker, barrel racing? With horses and mud and stuff?" Sam had jumped onto the big sofa. Her hands rested on the top of an overstuffed cushion, eyes wide with wonder and curiosity, seeming to have forgotten a delicate-looking ornament in her left hand.

"Yes, Sam. And could you please call me something besides Mr. Walker?"

"Well, Mom says once we meet somebody, if we like them, it's okay to make that somebody an honorary uncle or aunt. So, how about Uncle Caleb?"

He drew a long sip of the mimosa, wishing indeed that it were something stronger. "How about Uncle Cal?"

"Hooray, it's officially Christmas. We get a new uncle and aunt every year. It's way cool."

Cal had no idea what that meant, but it didn't seem the time to ask.

Jake grabbed the mimosa out of his hand. "Think maybe your new Uncle Cal needs something a little stronger than bubbles, Sam."

"You're a crack-up, Dad. How come everyone that meets us at Christmas needs something stronger? Mom makes the best cookies." Sam didn't seem to connect the dots between a strong drink and a killer cookie, which was fine with Cal. He accepted Jake's handoff of a hot coffee drink that smelled a lot like Irish whiskey.

"Come on around here, Cal." Liz patted the sofa. "And Sam, please be careful with the glass ornaments. You could cut your hand, or worse. Besides, that was your great-grandmother's." After handing off the cookies and rejected mimosa to Jake Sr., she'd swooped Ned out of some kind of jolly jumping cage. In it were bells and whistles, felt tufted birds, and mirrors, a place Cal thought too comfy to leave if a person wasn't yet two. But Ned giggled with delight at being in his mother's arms, so what did he know.

To be sure he could handle all this happy family stuff, he slugged a big portion of the now-cooling drink in his hand. Warmth spread to his veins as calm settled around his tense shoulders. "Thanks, Jake."

"So, you never had children. I'm sorry, Cal. They are a joy. It's not too late." She leaned in conspiratorially. "You see that handsome man, your boss, being tortured by a train set under that tree?"

"Yes." Indeed, it was hard to miss Jake Willis, who'd moved across the room and now worked to conquer something related to decorations. Willis, publisher, dad, successful, survivor of a horrible tragedy—at least Cal's research on his publisher supported that Jake lost his first wife in the South Tower eighteen years ago. Had it been that long? Now, lying on his side, linking track around a Christmas tree, his daughter hopped around from one foot to another, sticking ornaments on a fat blue spruce wherever they'd fit. Jake Jr. straddled his father's flank while the man tried to put an HO gauge engine on bent track. What made it more laughable was Eric 2 had come from behind the sofa, sneaking up on his dad, and sat on Jake's rear, with a hiccup and a word something close to "giddyup."

Cal felt only envy.

"Well, that gorgeous father of four was," she lowered her voice, "forty-something when I nabbed him."

He choked on the choice of words. "Nabbed?"

"Oh, silly. How else do you think two opposites end up together? It's a nab kind of thing. You know, Jake wanted me, needed me, but he was terrified." She smiled. "Of course, I can't say as I blame him." Liz reached behind her to the sofa table and pulled a silver-framed picture out for Cal's inspection.

"Who's the girl with pigtails, and…uh…kind of an odd wardrobe?"

"*Moi*. Yours truly. Me, Cal. That goofy wild woman is the one and only Lizzie Callahan. I snuck up on him and put that tree in his front yard. It's a selfie. Pretty good, right?"

"Is there some kind of allegorical tale here, Liz?"

From beneath the tree, Jake raised his head. "Ya think?"

She giggled and dumped Ned in Cal's lap. "Hold the monster. I'm going to get chips and dip. The game started about five minutes ago." She leaned over the coffee table and grabbed a remote, clicked the big flat-screen against the wall beside the tree to on, then grabbed Cal's mug, heading for the kitchen.

"Foooootbaaallll." Sammy Willis jumped onto the sofa, sinking in next to Cal. She pinched her baby brother's cheeks and yelled, "Mom, Ned stinks like poop."

"No surprise," Jake mumbled, clicking the last pieces of track together. He and Jake Jr. carefully placed the engine, two freight-type cars, and a caboose on the track. "Eric, do not stand up until I say it's okay. You ready, Jake?"

"Yes, sir."

Together, father and son turned the switch. The small train began a journey around the tree, which made Jake Jr. jump. With the second sense of fatherhood, Jake Sr. reached around and grabbed Eric 2 before the boy could trample the track. Cal wondered why Jake Jr. had asked to replace the broken train from Santa. Cal's boss lay back on the floor, staring at the ceiling, raising Eric about his shoulders and whispered, "Thank you, Jesus."

Nostalgia he'd never experienced punched Cal in the gut. Foster care sucked, and it had taken several years to track down his only sister. Thank God they'd connected, and after sharing life stories, they'd recognized similarities and managed to ease back into a loving sibling relationship.

Reminiscing had to wait as Liz returned and handed Cal a fresh coffee drink. She walked around to the coffee table and placed a tray with a bowl of chips and dip down for the taking. Good. He needed some food to go with the warm whiskey.

"Be right back. We need to talk." Her voice echoed down the hall as she raised her youngest son in the air. "You stink, Noodle."

Sammy held the chips and dip in her lap, snuggling against Cal's right side as if he were her real uncle. "Chip?"

"I'm Cal, but sure."

Sam giggled. "That's a knee slapper." Cal melted. Maybe he could be a dad, after all. "You should let me do it. I know precisely how much dip goes on what size chip to create the perfect taste sensation."

"Uh, okay." What six-year-old child used words like "precisely" and "taste sensation"? A Jake and Liz Willis kid. Sammy popped a chip into his mouth.

"Perfect, right?"

"I'm not going to argue with an expert, Sam."

"You're funny, Uncle Cal." She gave him a big toothy grin and a balled fist punched his arm. Noise from the big screen caught her attention. "Hey, it's your team."

"So it is." He stared at the TV, uncaring of the plays or any scoring. Contentment he couldn't explain washed over him as the girl started to snooze on his shoulder. Meantime, the younger Jake had saddled up next to him and squeezed between the sofa arm and Cal's hip on the other side. When he felt the boy's stare, Cal turned and looked into Jake's upturned face. "You okay, kid?"

"Yes, sir. I think I like the Cowboys."

"Good thing, since you are one."

The boy rested his head and laid a hand on Cal's knee. Sam snored softly on his other side. His boss stood, smiled, and tucked a droopy-eyed Eric 2 on the other side of his daughter. "I'm going to check on Liz. Be right back."

Cal was near hypnotized by the train chug-chug-chugging around the tree, with the game in the background a kind of white noise. Something about the entire vibe of the Willis household calmed every ounce of anxiety he'd ever felt.

He was almost dozing when Sam moved beside him. "Mom has a plan, you know, she always does, Uncle Cal. Sure hope you like Auntie Kate."

Her eyes closed again, and Cal couldn't help but smile. It seemed he had indeed fallen into some sort of conspiracy. Well, if Kate O'Malley was caught in the same web, he didn't mind. In fact, for the first time in too many years to count, Caleb Jethro Walker placed a bet. But not on the game. Nope. He was laying odds that Liz Willis's legendary skills at matchmaking would make the Super Bowl.

Chapter 12

So much for Cowboy-Santa-Jerk showing up. Kate looked at the clock on the oven. 4:40. *It's not like he promised breakfast, brunch, or even a late lunch.* He said he'd see her, and being stupid about the whole thing, she'd made a lasagna. It was nothing special, only cottage cheese, sauce out of a can, ground beef from the freezer, a lot of garlic, and cook-in-the-pan pasta. Figuring her writer for a no-show, she went ahead and set the aluminum pan in the oven. It was timed to start at 350 degrees for twenty minutes, and after that she lowered the temperature to keep it from drying out.

As a testament to her lack of experience with men, it dawned that no worldly woman would take the phrase "I'll see ya…" and prepare a meal around that slender thread of hope. Hope for what? At sixteen—when boys should have started to matter—Kate had decided that she didn't want anything to do with the opposite sex. Although her mother's profession might have had something to do with it, there was no solid reason for Kate to be petrified of sex. But there it was, an admission she could no longer run from, not after the subway encounter and last night's kiss.

Hell, that wasn't just kissing.

Kate re-centered her thinking to the present. If he did show up, it would be casual. But to be certain she wasn't devoured by anxiety, she'd put another bottle of Chardonnay in the fridge and set a bottle of red on the counter. She liked the no-corkscrew variety. The handy twist cap made her life easy. Yeah, easy to drink like a fish.

What if her writer was a wine snob? Okay, he had to show up first, so she kicked yet another concern from her head.

And if Caleb Walker were at the door, how would she handle his appearance?

I can open with the book.

It was memorable, and Kate conceded Liz had picked a winner. It was also intensely sexual, both in tension and the real thing. Kate had to get up and walk around the room in a few places. Too bad she hadn't waited to clean the house, because focused physical activity might have relieved the heat that simmered under her skin with each page.

Twice she'd had to put down the book and go for a walk. The first time, the chilly air bolstered her resolve and cooled the temperature of her blood.

Damn, cowboy. Who knew you had it in you?

About two hundred pages in, Kate knew what she loosely labeled as nervous energy would best be contained by moving. As a light rain fell, she went out a second time and headed to Saul's Market for a coffee. The friendly store was more like a highway mini-mart, stocked with essentials—chocolate, aspirin, tampons, canned spaghetti sauce, chips, cheese, rice, pasta, tortillas, a small area of fresh produce, and a corner devoted to items essential to the practice of his Jewish faith. He also stocked a healthy amount of wine, beer, and spirits. Although Kate had never been to the back cooler, the locals knew that their smiling, if rounded, proprietor kept a stash of select fine wines and all manner of celebratory fare in the back.

She loved her little market. There was always somebody in the store, and Saul had a penchant for drawing people into conversation, so social misfits, as Kate often considered herself, could make an acquaintance or two.

"Miss Kate, welcome. I was afraid you'd forget me over the holidays."

"Saul, silly man. That'll never happen." She smiled. "I was going to have coffee, but can you make me a hot chocolate? Large."

"For you, my best editor, extra chocolate with whip cream."

"Yum, perfect."

He busied himself at a machine, looking over his shoulder when the bell jingled over the door. "Abraham, welcome, how are you, how's your wife?" Returning his attention to the hot chocolate creation, he shouted over the noise, "You know Kate?"

"I don't think I do, Saul. Hi." The newcomer was good-looking, with kind eyes and a welcoming smile, but married. "Nice to meet you. I go by Abe."

"Kate."

Idle chat about the weather and the upcoming holidays didn't bother Kate because it equaled contact with another life form outside of the office. She was happy for the break.

"Your mega-chocolate is ready, Kate."

"Saul, you're a gem." She put down a ten-dollar bill. "Keep the change, or put it in the tip jar for your employees."

"Sure. That's nice. You have plans for the holidays, Kate?"

Abe had disappeared down the aisle that had a small selection of baby food.

"Only some editing, Saul."

"That's not good. You should find someone to spend some time with, enjoy Christmas."

"I should. But I've got you, Saul."

He laughed. "I'm going to keep my eye out for you, Kate."

"You always do." She tugged the glove she'd removed to pay for the drink back onto her right hand. Daring a sip through the opening in the cup lid, she said, "A little heaven right here on earth, Saul. Thank you." She shouted at the corner of the store where Abe had disappeared. "Nice meeting you."

The bell jingled over the door again, and Saul turned his attention to another customer. Kate could stay and extend her foray into civilization, but now, encouraged to finish her job, she slipped out the door. Kate loved the rain, being in it, watching it fall. The outing had refreshed and encouraged her to finish reading Santa-Cowboy's book.

***

She looked at the clock again. Two hours had passed since her foray to the corner market. She'd finished the book and begun editing in earnest. Kate had done everything humanly possible to erase the feelings Cal Walker's writing had triggered. And it wasn't the book. She'd already been attracted to him, so much so it pissed her off. Enough that she'd foolishly downed two glasses of Chardonnay, because, well, damn, if he didn't show up, why drink red. She didn't like red except in a pinch. He wasn't going to show.

Why would he?

Because he kissed me.

She knew she was damaged goods, and he'd probably been disappointed by her kiss. Prim, uptight Katherine Mary O'Malley did not have a reputation as being a so-called hot babe.

Screw it. She pulled her creation from the oven and peeled back the foil, checking for dryness. "Damn." Kate reached to fill a measuring cup with water from the sink but stopped. "Wait, I've got an idea." She unscrewed the cap from the red wine and poured some into the measuring cup. Slowly draining the wine over the top of the pasta, she re-covered the pan and placed it back in the oven.

"That should do it." Looking around, she said, "Where was I?" The book sat in judgment from the dining table where'd she'd moved to facilitate making margin notes, etc. The chairs were a little less comfortable, but that would keep her on her toes. "Back to it, Kate."

Halfway to the table, Kate determined that to finish editing the book without being too close-minded about Cal Walker's style, she should have another glass of wine. She returned to the project on the table, realizing the lamp over behind the chair and closer to the window seat might offer better lighting. *Liar.* She wanted to watch the street for the cowboy. Distracted for a second, she sipped the wine and watched as the rain shifted to big snowflakes. It might stay on the ground, it might not, but leaning her head against the glass, resigned to another holiday alone, she took comfort from the Christmas vignettes in the windows across from her building.

***

Cal felt inept. He was also cold. A good coat didn't completely insulate when rain turned first to sleet, and then snow. It was stupid, his plan. He was standing below Kate's second-story apartment, beneath a timid canopy—one designed only to allow someone to open a door or be admitted quickly after the buzzer sounded. It was not meant to keep an indecisive man holding a small Christmas tree, a packaged train set, and a bottle of ridiculously expensive champagne protected from the elements only by a paper bag.

He could afford the bubbly. Cost was never an issue, not since his stock market successes of fifteen years ago. He looked down at his Apple watch and smiled. But none of the financial success mattered. He no longer cared about the book. Okay, not entirely true, but making it as a writer paled in comparison to what he'd experienced in Jake and Liz Willis's living room. Family, an undeniable connection between two adults who were still in love with each other and who adored their children. And what about those kids? Well-adjusted, happy, inquisitive, silly siblings. The specter of his foster-care years threatened, it always did, but Cal tamped it back into the dark reaches of his brain.

His past didn't matter, and his future wasn't possible if Kate rejected him.

He was banking on Liz Willis's proclamation as she walked him to the elevator two hours ago. "She likes you, Cal. She's scared, shy, but she likes you." The elevator doors had closed on those words, after which he managed to make FAO Schwartz and a corner tree lot before the weather turned nasty. The champagne had been a little tougher. He'd been disappointed when he walked into the corner market and looked around. Cal feared he'd have to settle for boxed wine and corn nuts. He wasn't even going to ask until the gray-mustachioed owner walked out from behind a cooler.

"Can I help you, son?"

"Well, sir, thanks for the compliment, but I've logged a lot of miles on the back of a horse, kind of ridden hard and put up wet, you know?"

"Ah."

"You know, I've heard that 'ah' expression before. Most recently from a young woman who lives down the street."

"That would mean you're Kate's sort-of cowboy-Santa."

Cal should have known. The quiet, often severe, Marion-the-Librarian-type he'd fallen for had a friend in the local grocer. She lived by herself, and she was lonely. She must be, given the walls she'd built to protect herself from everything. Despite putting barriers up against most of the world, it made sense that at the very least, Kate would have some acquaintances in her neighborhood. He was surprised that she'd shared a confidence with the man.

"Busted, I guess. To be fair, I'm a real cowboy and a fake Santa."

"Does it matter which is which? Seems to me that if she likes the cowboy, she likes the Santa, or vice versa."

"Guess not. But I'd still like to ride up on a good horse, and…well, you know, sweep her off her feet."

"You writers."

"We writers have to keep our editors happy, right? And I'm a businessman and rancher first, Mr....?"

"In this store, it's Saul."

"So the sign says, but I wouldn't be so presumptuous."

"I give you permission, rancher."

"It's Caleb. Most call me Cal."

"Cal it is. What brings you to my humble establishment?"

"You may not carry it, but I'd like champagne. Preferably the good stuff."

"As it happens, I cater to weddings." He pointed to a small sign behind him, "Ask about our catering services." "We don't place the better choices on the floor though, no sense in inviting some desperate yuppie to rip me off. You thinking French or a California sparkling?"

"Saul, you've restored my faith in local merchants."

"It's New York City. Small markets and eateries are standard, but I try to keep this place a step above packaged cupcakes and rotgut wine."

"Every day I'm here, I learn something new to like. Thanks. As to a champagne choice, I'd prefer French."

Cal ended up with a Louis Roderer and fudge ripple ice cream. After all, he didn't want Kate to go hungry. That is, if she let him in the door.

When he left, Saul winked. "It's good you remembered dessert."

Cal wondered if the comment was a hint. "I'm sorry?"

"Ice cream makes everybody happy."

"I see." Cal didn't. Still, it was obvious Saul knew his neighborhood well enough to insinuate something good might come of delivering a dessert to Kate. Thanking Saul, he trotted out to his waiting cab, making the half-block to Kate's building in New York style, brooking no arguments from the bad weather. The cabbie slammed to a stop directly in front of the brownstone. Cal would have tipped generously anyway, but it was nice of the driver to help him get his Kate-bribes up and under the inefficient overhang.

He'd paced a bit, despite the snow, even went back across the street to catch a glimpse of her apartment. The lights were on. He walked between parked cars, over snow-dusted blacktop, and settled beneath the overhang at the entrance to the building.

All he had to do was ring the buzzer.
Except he was petrified.

Chapter 13

Kate heard the buzzer through the self-induced fog in her brain. She also smelled her meal. The lasagna was still alive, thank goodness, because she needed to eat something. She should celebrate saving the day by keeping the dish moist with another glass of wine. With the covered dish safely on the counter, she turned off the oven and partook of her prize. Chardonnay, gold and inviting, stared at her from the glass. The annoying doorbell from below sounded again.

Six-twenty p.m. *When did I sit down?*

It didn't matter. What counted now was who—whom?—was at the door and whether she should answer. She leaned against the doorframe and pushed the microphone button. "Who's there?"

"Santa Claus."

Right. It sounded like one of those comedy skits on SNL. The show ran reruns of long-ago seasons on a local station. She watched it religiously. After all, in her opinion, the show belonged to New Yorkers. So she guessed that made her a snob.

"Landshark?" Would he bite?

"Candygram." The response whispered through the intercom sent Kate into a fit of giggles. He was a *Saturday Night Live* guy. *Yeah.* She hit the door release button with her palm and waited. There were heavy footsteps on the stairs. *Geeze, did I let in the boogeyman?* But she knew who it was. Cowboy-Santa-Landshark had big feet.

She wondered if the old saying was true, big feet, big…

"Kate?" A knock she should ignore. A man she should run from. Writer-Santa-Cowboy-Cal was standing on the other side of her door when he should be somewhere on the other side of the country, branding a cow or something, and she was mad at him. "Who is this? Seriously."

"It's me."

"Pray tell, who is me?"

"You know damned well, Katie. I'm cold, the snow on my coat has melted so I'm wet, and my arms are tired."

"Ba-dump. You fly in?"

"What?"

"You know, I flew in, and boy are my arms tired?" She shouldn't be enjoying this weird through-a-door conversation. She'd read his book, loved the book. Now she had to figure out how to tell the tall, handsome cowboy on the other side of the door. It was an admission she hadn't expected to make. And it meant Cal would win the benefit of his bargain. Except they hadn't agreed on enough specifics in terms of her finishing and liking the book. She would edit it, but he had no reason to stick around and bug her as promised should she not be able to get through an additional eighty-five pages.

All of which made her feel sad, like she was losing something. No, not a thing, a person. A man. Caleb Walker would have no reason to hang around and taunt, touch, or kiss her again. Once she accepted the idea that the empty feeling connected to his going back to Texas was wrapped up in feelings for the man. Kate blushed. The cause of the rushing sound between her ears, her heart pounding as if she'd run up the stairs, the flush she felt, was all due to the man waiting out on her threshold.

"I'm not only wet and cold, Katie. I'm hungry too."

"Oh, well. Why didn't you say so?" She yanked open the door, unaware that her cowboy-writer-Santa had placed his weight against it. Cal toppled through and down. A big box slid across the floor, stopping at the area rug's edge. A bag marked "Saul's" rolled toward the kitchen, and the man—*God you are gorgeous, writer-Santa-dude*—lay on his back, clutching another bag as if life itself depended on it.

"What the hell?"

Kate dropped to her knees beside Cal. "I'm so sorry. I had no idea you were letting my door hold you up like that."

"My arms were full, and I'd been outside for about half an hour."

"You're a stalker?"

"I wasn't stalking. Shit, Kate, that's mean. And why were my arms full, or why was I on your front stoop for thirty minutes, braving the elements?"

"Yes."

"Because I brought you champagne and ice cream, and because I was scared."

"Oh goodness, that doesn't seem possible. You, cowboy-Santa, you frightened?"

"If you say, 'of little ol' me,' I'm going to forget my manners, Kate."

"Katie."

Cal stared at her, his eyes going from skeptical to warm, soft, and interested. She wanted to brush the hair that had fallen over his forehead back into place, which was silly because in truth, she wanted to touch more of him than a few strands on his head. "I've decided it's okay, anyone who brings me champagne and ice cream, well, there are concessions to be made. Plus, good thing it's freezing outside, I mean, on account of the ice cream."

He grinned, and rolled, resting the side of his face against the palm of his right hand. "What kind of concessions?"

"Oh, like calling me Katie."

"Okay, and what else?"

"Nothing else I can think of, not right now anyway."

Cal took her left hand in his and rubbed a thumb gently back and forth across her wrist. "So, there may be more?"

"More what?"

"Help me up, Katie."

She stood and held out both arms to help. His grip was strong, but that didn't surprise her. However, the fluidity with which he went from prone to standing was nothing short of astonishing. "Wow. I guess all that cattle rustling and stuff is good for your leg muscles." The minute the words left her mouth, she felt the flush of embarrassment from her forehead to her toes.

"Ma'am, I don't steal cattle, I raise 'em."

"Oh, sorry. I guess rustling's the wrong word."

"Sure fills a man with a lot of confidence about your editing skills, Ms. O'Malley."

"I kind of like Katie better."

"Well now, that's an interesting admission. And a ranch is hard work. I have a lot of muscle tone. Want I should take off my shirt and show you?"

She tried to pull away, knowing full well that roping and stuff made his arms strong, and in all likelihood other parts of his body.

He hadn't let go, and now he was doing that thumb brush-thing across both of her wrists. Heat raced up her arms from the points of contact, and from there, down her spine, and as if betrayed by tissue, vessels, and nerve endings, settled with a warmth in parts of her anatomy she fought against acknowledging.

Kate thought for sure he would kiss her, but instead an even bigger smile broke out on his face. "I brought you a present, well, two actually." Cal bent, picked up the bag he'd held securely when falling, and placed it on the bar. He reopened the door. "Here, hold it open for a second." He gave her a stern stare. "Don't lock me out."

"Nope."

She watched as he dashed down the stairs, hearing noises she couldn't quite make sense of, but then he came bounding back, this time holding a small tree, with a stand on it no less.

"You like?" Cal brushed past her and Kate's senses captured the aroma of pine. She'd forgotten how good a live tree smelled. A haphazard string of lights was wrapped around the little tree, the cord end of the plug dangling in anticipation for a socket.

"Where would you like me to plug this in, ma'am?"

She let the form of address go, even though he'd used it twice already. She'd have to think about a snappy comeback, but the tree was such a sweet gesture, she capitulated. "Well, it's small. How about the dining table?"

He glanced from her to the table and back. "You'll see it, and…" He walked over to the table, holding the tree above it by about a foot. "There's enough room around the sides."

"Enough room for what? I can always eat at the bar for a few weeks." Or on the sofa. She was embarrassed to mention the TV trays in the hall closet. The idea that she ate in front of the TV all the time was too big a reveal into her loneliness.

"You have a sheet?"

"Sure." She was a sheet freak but no need to let Cal know that.

"Well?"

"What?"

"The sheet. Snap to it, Ms. O'Malley. At this moment, you are officially a Christmas Elf, and I get to order elves around." Kate snorted, but some kind of crazy joy had gurgled up from within, and she laughed to the linen closet and back. "One sheet as ordered, Santa, sir." She saluted him and almost melted into a puddle on the floor at his responding smile. Her knees felt weak enough that she pulled out the barstool to watch him work.

"Want I should shoot your coat and hat again, cowboy?"

The wet coat flew in her direction, the hat seconds behind.

***

Maybe forty minutes had passed, during which time Cal watched Kate out of the corner of his eye. The champagne sat in an ice bucket on the counter. He hadn't dared open it after the tumble through the door and onto her floor. It could wait, and Kate seemed content to leave her half-empty Chardonnay glass on the coffee table in front of the TV.

The Bishop's Wife, another oldie, was playing but she'd again muted the sound. He enjoyed the quiet, careful not to fill it with chitchat. Cal had accepted that he wanted Kate in his life, and he didn't need to complicate this special moment with nonsense. Besides, the snowfall outside made its own unique kind of silence. Peaceful without and within, he'd plugged in the tree, rearranged the lights a bit, wrapped the sheet under the stand and around it, a mound of white.

She'd eyed him quizzically when he picked up the FAO Schwartz bag. "You'll see," he said. "Now either close your eyes or take a nap."

"I'm going to take a shower. I meant to after cleaning house today, and then I fell asleep." Kate grinned. "Reading your book."

"Snarky."

"Teasing."

"You didn't read it?" But she'd disappeared down the hall, and hearing the bedroom door lock, he went back to the chore of setting up an electric train to circle the small tree. Twenty-two pieces of track later, the black engine was chugging around the fragrant pine in an oblong-shaped route, clearing the edge of the table by two inches on both sides. He'd paid for the set with extras, and Santa's Shop with lights shining from within now sat snuggled into the sheet. There were some signals and a few frosted fir trees of various shapes and sizes. The set even came with elves that hooked onto the caboose, and a Santa figurine that fit into the engine compartment. He only wished the store had a Santa with a cowboy hat.

After opening the champagne and pouring two glasses, he couldn't resist a sip. He lifted his glass to the tree. "Congrats, Caleb Walker. Not only have you gone round the bend, but you're also acting a bit childlike. So be it."

"I think childlike is better than brutish, manly, macho, etc., cowboy-Santa."

"Katie." He'd been too self-absorbed to hear the bedroom door open, but he should have smelled her when she approached quietly from behind.

"It's so sweet. And a train? Holy cow, you may have made my day, no, my holiday. Thanks, Cal."

Her shoulder leaned in against his, and he knew she was staring at the tree and watching the train go around. Like the other day, Kate smelled of soap, but this time he recognized undertones of citrus, maybe lemon? Macho Cal Walker. That he could ferret out her scent didn't make him less of a man. He held still, enjoying the slight pressure of Kate's body against his, mere inches between them. Moving meant breaking the spell.

He felt rather than saw her lift the glass to her lips and take a sip. "Holy tasty, Batman, that's amazing stuff."

Cal turned. "I hoped you'd like it. It seemed worthwhile to enjoy a little holiday spirit before you raked me over the coals about the book. Did you read the whole thing?"

Her eyes sparkled in the dim light from the pendants over the bar, the tree, and the glow of the television. "Maybe. What does the J in CJ stand for anyway?"

"Jethro."

Kate seemed to fight spitting her last sip of champagne out in a guffaw. After a second, she stared him straight on. "Are you shitting me?"

"You know, Ms. O'Malley, for an editor, you seem a bit short in the articulation department."

"Well, yes, that's probably true but then, I've never met a Jethro before."

"I'm not 'a Jethro.' My name is Caleb Jethro Walker. That's all I got. You can see why I used CJ for the book."

"Hmm, I could see why you'd use it for everything."

"You're going to make me cry, Katie."

"I'm sorry. It's not like me to be mean. A lot of people at work think I am, mean that is, but mostly it's because I've always been, you know, shy, uptight…there's a lot of adjectives I've heard walking into the lunch break room."

He turned away from the tree, hating the way she was treated, loving the furrow lines on her brow, the slight pout to her lips, loving Kate. Uncertain how to bridge the gap between them, their personalities and styles, he kissed her nose. "Bunch of rattlesnakes, Katie. I'll come over anytime you want and bag 'em up."

"What does one do with bagged rattlers, CJ?"

"Barbecue 'em. Little hot sauce, some grilled onion and green peppers. Mighty fine eats, gal."

He half expected Kate to punch him, but she didn't break away from his closeness. Her eyes closed and he could sense the tremulousness at their closeness, so he leaned back from her and took the glass from her hand. "This is great stuff. How about a little more?"

"I thought you were starving."

"Well, don't look, but there might be a few fork-size bites out of that delicious casserole thing you left sitting on the sink. Took the edge off a little."

She laughed aloud. "Yes, to the champagne." She reached up, and her fingers plucked at something on his collar. "And the spaghetti sauce stain on your collar gave you up. You want some dinner, Santa?"

Her words were spoken into his shirt. The vibration against the fabric rattled Cal, enough that he had to turn. Irresistible. He tugged her with one hand toward the bar and carefully placed the glasses down to pull her closer. "In bed. I want dinner in bed."

Cal studied her reaction to the suggestion. Her green eyes shone with desire, something he hadn't expected. Teasingly, he tugged the ponytail gently to force her face up. Her hair remained damp, which for some reason he found sexy as hell. "You got all dressed up, Kate."

"Booger."

"Just an observation, ma'am." He used the knot tied in an oversize flannel shirt to pull Kate's hips against him. It might take calculus to get her out of the form-fitting jeans, and no kidding, the Smurf slippers were back.

"Where we have dinner doesn't matter, but can it wait a little bit?"

He could see she wasn't coy, realizing that it could destroy their budding relationship if he took this moment to the next level. But what relationship would they have if the physical attraction was ignored? They'd spontaneously combust in an elevator somewhere and kill hundreds of people. He chuckled at the thought.

"You're laughing at me." Kate pushed to free herself, but Caleb was too quick. He spun her back into his arms.

"I'm not laughing at you, Katie, but you are adorable. No, there was something in my head that was pretty funny."

"Writers are weird."

"Hmm," he kissed her forehead, her nose, then nibbled on one ear and moved his mouth down her long neck, "terrible people, us writers." Now he knew it was her turn to experience the buzz of words spoken against skin. "Editors, on the other hand, editors are the glue that keeps a writer from spinning off."

"God, that feels amazing."

"What? Whispering in your ear, or this?" Cal moved his hand up the inside of her shirt, no bra, good girl, Katie. "Or this?" He cupped her breast and circled a thumb around one nipple. The guttural release that escaped her stepped Cal's hard-on up a notch to damned near painful. "Or this?" He moved his other hand and untied the loose knot in her shirt, pulling it aside, "You're beautiful." His mouth lowered and he flicked his tongue across her other breast, tugging on the now-rock-like nipple gently.

"I can't do this."

He should slow his pace, uncertain of what frightened her. "Yes." His thumb continued to circle. "You can."

She shook her head back and forth. "I'm no good at it, Cal. It's useless." Again, she tried to free herself from his hold, but the effort was now lukewarm.

"Why would you say that, sweetheart?"

"Haven't you heard? I'm a prude, an uptight spinster."

"Honey, you've been reading too many historical romances." But he slowed his approach, kissing her nose. "Have you tried," he caught her gaze, "anything contemporary lately?"

She pushed her palms against his shoulders, but her eyes smoldered, the green rim of color barely showing around darkened pupils. "I'm not…" a frightened hiccup, "not good at sex."

"Come on, Kate. A little practice is all you need." He blew in her ear, then brushed his mouth along her freckles, finding her lips. He broke the kiss, staying nose to nose. "I couldn't shoot the side of a big rig from ten feet for a long time."

"Practice?"

"Practice."

"There's nothing wrong with me?"

"Haven't seen all of you yet, darlin', but I expect not."

He kissed her slowly, and she muttered against his lips, "Practice."

How the woman in his arms could ever have thought she failed at a physical relationship with a man was beyond him. "Practice." He held her against his chest, and she relaxed against his shirt. After a few minutes, he turned her and rested her back against him, his chin on the top of her head, so they could stare at the tree and listen to the rhythmic circling of the train as it chug-chug-chugged in circles.

"I think I can, I think I can."

"What's that from?" Kate mumbled.

"A children's book. *The Little Engine…*"

"*That Could.*" She exhaled deeply against him, and Cal felt the slight quiver where his hands rested against her skin. Cal couldn't tolerate the situation much longer so he either had to leave or go all in. As if on automatic, his hands traveled up her belly, thumbs and index fingers once again circled her breasts, slowly, lightly grazing her skin.

"Oh my goodness."

Cal shifted and turned her around to face him again, noticing her eyes wide open with delight. "My goodness? Really?"

"Yes, really." Kate tucked her fingers inside his belt and tugged his shirt free, her hands roaming slowly over his skin up to his chest. "Two can play, Cal."

"One would hope…" She went to work unbuttoning his shirt and pulling it away from his shoulders. Suddenly he was glad for his years of demanding work on the ranch, tan, and trim. Forty-something or not, he was comfortable with and without clothes.

"You are a good writer, CJ Walker. I wouldn't think sitting at a computer all day would build muscles."

"Flattery, Ms. Editor? It's riding, roping, and bailing hay, ma'am."

She flicked his pants below the belt buckle. "You lift bales of hay with this?" Kate squeezed his erection through the fabric. Not only was Cal shocked at her aggression, but her touch uncapped any restraint he'd managed to this point. Lifting her in his arms, he moved her the few feet to the sofa. Setting her down, he flipped first one, then the other Smurf slipper over the top of the couch.

"My slippers."

"No whining." He grinned. "And that's not all, Madam Editor, that's not all." He tugged her blue jeans off and spread her thighs apart with his hands. "Did you read the book, Katie?"

"No." She was lying, he was pretty sure anyway, so he ran a finger up her inner thigh and slipped it beneath her panties. "You sure you didn't even read a few more pages?"

"I didn't."

"If you didn't, I have to stay."

"Please," she shuddered at his touch, "don't go."

His finger dipped inside her and the heat there nearly brought him to a climax. He took a deep breath and checked himself. "I think you read it." With each word, he moved his finger in and out of her. "In. Fact. I. Think. You. Read. Some. Of. The. Really. Hot. Parts."

"I didn't, I swear."

Cal rested his mouth against her thigh and tugged the fabric to one side until his tongue found her most sensitive spot. "You sure you didn't read a little of my book, sweetheart?"

"Uhm…"

"I bet you did." For a few minutes, he said nothing further, instead speaking volumes in her most sensitive area. Kate was writhing beneath him, and her hands found the back of his head. He looked up for a second, needing to see her face when she came. "Admit it, Kate," his finger slid in and out faster, his thumb on her hardened clitoris, "you read it."

"Yes, yes, yes, I read your damn book." Her back stiffened, and she shuddered from her head to her toes. "I read it and, God forgive me, I loved it." She collapsed back onto the sofa, her breathing coming in jagged bursts, residual shivers shaking her body beneath his touch. "Caleb."

"Yes, ma'am?"

"Do you have a condom?"

"More than one."

"Figures. It was in your book, you know." A lazy smile, encouraging him.

She'd read it, all right. He might write erotica to the tenth power, but he made sure his characters were safe, damned safe. He kicked off his shoes, unable to stand the ache in his groin another second. He pulled a condom from his pocket and then kicked one pant leg off before tearing the wrapper with his teeth. Slipping the silky material on, he stopped.

"Please, Cal."

"Are you sure, ma'am?"

She punched his gut, presumably for the "ma'am" bit. "Practice, Cal. Practice." Then she pulled him inside her.

"Katie…" The heat was unbearable, and Cal knew he'd have to make it up to her later, because in an instant, he lost control. He burst with pent-up emotion and something about Kate. He already loved her, but the climax sealed his commitment. He'd never felt so raw, so needing, as he did around Kate O'Malley. "Sweet mother-of-pearl."

"You're funny, writer-Santa-boy."

"I owe you a long, slow lovemaking, O'Malley."

"Sure. But now that we got past that initial stuff, we can eat lasagna and drink champagne, and…"

Cal raised himself up against her on the sofa and kissed her on the mouth. She didn't flinch. The heady, sweet taste of lovemaking was unforgettable. He tried to instill promise in the kiss. That he wouldn't let her down, do what they'd done and then disappear. He muttered into her neck, "Did you say lasagna?"

"I did."

"Is that what that casserole thing is?" He was getting used to Kate now, managing to deflect the punch. "First, I'd like to thank you for the last fifteen minutes."

"You're welcome. I guess that was pretty hot."

He pulled himself up and tugged her into the crook of his arm, staring down at his half-on, half-off pants. "I thought you editors had a lot of multisyllabled words at your beck and call."

"Okay, that was steamin' hot?"

"Indeed it was, Kate. Indeed it was."

"In fact, Mr. Walker, I'd venture the supposition—big word that—what we did was hotter than your book."

"You think?" Cal kissed the top of Kate's head. "Well, let's see about that after dinner. I'll read the good stuff aloud to you." Kate spun out of his reach, found her underwear, and slipping them back up to her belly button, jumped up from the sofa. She looked adorable. Her shyness showed through, and she quickly buttoned the flannel shirt.

"Hey."

"Hey, what?"

"You really did get me a train?"

"I got you a train."

"It's lovely."

"Well, I mean, Kate, it's a train."

"I was going to say some gooey thanks earlier, but…"

"But?"

"Well, we uh, you know, we…"

"Did the deed? I liked you prim and all proper, Katie, but I got to say, that other you, the slide-off-the-couch girl, the moans-beautifully girl, that one should come out more often." As soon as he said it, Cal saw she was embarrassed. Ashamed even of her own sexuality. He didn't want to push her on it now, but it was important. Certainly, if they were going to become a thing, they had to open up to each other. So he dove in first. "I was a foster-child."

Her mouth dropped. "You're kidding, right?"

"Well, since we've stepped up the relationship, I think it's fair to start revealing our pasts, the terrors, the insecurities, idiosyncrasies, things that have hurt us, made us happy, you know, all that stuff."

"Okay."

"So?"

Kate went to the bar and slugged the Louis Roderer. "My mom was a hand model."

"No kidding?"

"Scout's honor."

"I lived in thirteen different homes between the ages of twelve and seventeen." He saluted to give validity to his admission.

She smiled at him as if genuinely happy to share his past. He knew these little snippets barely scratched the surface but felt it was important, so he didn't object when she refilled their glasses, handing him one. "And…"

"And?"

"You're only the second person I've ever been with. And that thing that you did to me? I've never felt anything like it. God," she seemed terrified again, "I hope I wasn't terrible."

Cal felt gut-punched and a little sick. Everything she'd said, her behavior whenever they'd met, the amount she drank to stay in the room with him, it should have been like a first grade primer. Huge print, double spaced. See Kate shy away. See Kate drink wine to look Cal in the eyes. See Kate shiver at the slightest physical contact.

He leaned in, kissing her neck, then whispered in her ear, "You were incredible, Katie O'Malley. It's all I can do not to…" Cal kissed her on the lips, then held up his glass. "A toast to our secrets then."

"Hear, hear." Kate took a deep breath, and with a blush, seemed intent on sharing something else. An involuntary shiver shook her, and it rocked him. He wanted to hold her, and promise her she didn't need to say anything more. Except she looked him straight on, held up her glass. "And here's to my mom, stage name of Wendy Avalon."

"I don't think I've heard of her."

"Well, that's probably because she wasn't mainstream film, Cal." Kate took a deep breath. "My mom was a porn star."

Chapter 14

Cal hadn't planned on leaving Kate and not showing up the next day. But the text from Will in Texas put him in a terrible position in terms of the ranch. He had to go back. Plus, in the safe, behind emergency cash, an antique Colt 45, and the only pictures he had of his family, was a certain item that had suddenly become valuable to Cal. For too many years, he'd thought the small black box would be an asset listed in his trust. Not anymore.

He hadn't planned on falling in love with a stern, brilliant, funny, skinny girl who had more fire than Maggie Pollitt in Tennesse William's *Cat on a Hot Tin Roof*. It wasn't something she caught from her mother because the woman supported her only child by roles in blue movies. But it was no wonder Kate was so afraid of being with someone. It wasn't the sex, rather the fear that she would become her mother. His job, if she let him, was to heal the scars of Wendy Avalon's past.

For certain, Kate needed him, and he needed to help her understand that being sexual, and having sexuality, wasn't a curse. Not if you were in love. And Caleb Jethro Walker had discovered he was exactly that. Very much in love.

***

It was after six p.m. Thursday. Not Monday. Not Tuesday. Not Wednesday. But already Thursday. Without a single word from Cal.

Jackass.

Kate shouldn't have expected anything more or less from the man. She'd read his book, agreed it was great, gave it the big OKAY for publication, which of course meant subsequent edits, fine-tuning, etc. But it was good. She loved it.

But why?

It was full of vivid sexual encounters, so not up her alley. Still, Liz and Jake Willis were right. The characters grabbed in a way that wouldn't let go. Their pasts colliding sweetly and romantically, with a love they almost lost, and conflict, loads of good old conflict.

So, she'd fallen in love with the book.

Far worse, she'd fallen in love with the man.

And horrors of all horrors, she'd slept with him.

Shit, shit, triple shit.

Now he'd disappeared. Poof, gone.

Kate didn't dare appear desperate, so she'd nonchalantly asked Jake Willis if he expected to see Caleb Walker any time soon. An innocent enough question. Jake's response had been terse, as if there were some sort of conspiracy to hide the new writer out of town, isolate him from Kate O'Malley.

Maybe he'd called her? Her cell phone was still sitting in a baggie of rice on her kitchen sink. Pretty funny how it fell into the soapy dish water. Hilarious, right? Cal had been kissing his way up her neck, behind her ears, and when she'd spun suddenly, he picked her up, slamming her rear end onto the countertop. Oops had been the moment when the cellphone in her pocket had become cellphone in the china, rendering both flatware and cellphone useless. That moment had been the prelude to the second time they'd made love.

Well, he'd left nothing on her answering machine, and there were no little pink notes in her inbox at the office either, signifying someone had called for her.

Without apparent concern, she'd walk by Margie Quillan's desk and ask, "Any new messages for me?" And four days running, Margie shook her head left to right and returned to work on her desk. Kate was ashamed to admit she had no clue what Margie did for the company. It made Kate wonder if she was that shallow. She deserved all the whispers about her appearance, demeanor, and attitude. Kate O'Malley was as careless about other people's feelings as it appeared was the talented and handsome Rancher-Santa-Writer, Caleb Jethro Walker.

The tears that beckoned at the corners of her eyes would have to wait. *Screw you, Caleb.*

A new acquisition sat front and center, but Kate's neat, orderly desk suddenly appeared as empty and desolate as her life. She wanted a hole-punch, a stapler, a little dog-shaped dish filled with paperclips. She wanted an African violet that needed attention, sitting behind the computer screen. And an ice-cold beer. Kate longed for a foamy ale that left a ring on her desk. It would sit waiting, being there for a sip when she needed it, and when done, she could wipe away the ring of condensation with her sleeve. Like a cowgirl, after she finished the last gulp. Screw the cowboy fantasy. It would feel great to mess up the sleeve of an Ann Taylor bibbed blouse.

Damn. The only reason he wouldn't have called or showed up had to be because Kate had been a lousy lover. What other reason? Or maybe he'd only wanted to conquer the prissy editor and regale the conquest back in Texas. It didn't matter. She'd blown it.

Now Kate was sure she could never go back to being a dignified, dedicated editor. Cal had sucked her into his web. He'd taken her out of the carefully compartmentalized world of her feelings, a safe place, a place that kept her from thinking about her childhood, her mother. *God, Mom, a porn star? Really?*

She guessed it wasn't fair. Her mom had done the best she could. Hell, she'd managed to raise a nice, uptight, prudish book editor. That was something, except Kate had discovered sex with a cowboy. Irony made stories. So here she was, aching for physical contact, stuck between in love and heartbreak.

Did she imagine the knock at her office door? Would that she had the luxury of windows revealing activity outside her closed door. But it was late, and the main office entry was locked up. Everyone was at the office Christmas party.

But not Kate.

If it was Walker, if someone had let him in, she'd throw something at him, maybe her computer.

"Hey, Kate."

Matt. Yuck. "How are you, Matt? Merry almost Christmas."

"Good, and ditto on the salutation. How about you?"

"Fine, working." Hint. Hint. "New property to consider." Triple hint.

"I heard you ended up liking Caleb Walker's book."

"Yes, it's good. Should sell well when released next year."

"Hear you like the writer, too?"

"Pound sand, Matt."

"Well, your cheeks are rosy, and you seemed all happy and, dare I say it, satisfied when you came in on Monday."

"You're fishing, Matt. And it's none of your business how I feel, or whether you think I got laid somewhere along the line in the last week. Either way, the only thing that matters is you get the hell out of my office."

"Aw, Kate. Don't go all bitchy on me."

Again she wished she had some kind of weapon to bean him with, but her desk was its usual stoic spotless entity. She opted to ignore him instead, staring at a plaque on the opposite wall of her office.

"I broke it off with Mary."

"Whoopee for Mary. I'll send her a congratulatory note." Kate smiled at Matt and pointed at the door. "Your ship sailed years ago, boss. So could you please let me get back to work? And shouldn't you be at the office party? Oh gosh, too bad, did they throw you out? Well, there must be a holiday party you can crash somewhere."

"Probably. Thought I'd check in. Sorry the Santa thing didn't work out for you." Kate wanted to smack the leer off Matt's face but bit her lip instead. "Anyway, don't work too late."

"Thanks for the visit." He walked down the hall, and her limited view couldn't guarantee it, but hopefully, out the door to the elevators. "Don't party too hard. Hah." The asshole hadn't even shut the door to her office.

The encounter had worsened her spirits. Kate was ready to steal Christmas from someone. Not Whoville, of course, that had been done. But Matt's hovering and innuendo had done nothing to help Kate out of her funk. No kidding. Of all the people in the world she could go another ten years without seeing—no, a lifetime—Matt would be in the top ten. Maybe even number one.

She pulled the manuscript closer and grabbed a pencil from the desk drawer. Jake had dropped the new submission off before leaving the office. The conversation was brief, friendly, and not a word about the status of one CJ Walker. "Liz thinks you'll like this one, Kate. Give it a go for me, okay?"

She remembered mumbling something like, sure, but that had been well over two hours earlier. She'd been frozen with a sadness that seemed impossible to bear, and then the fun visit from Matt.

Kate knew she had to do something, might as well be work as stomp around her apartment in tears. *Been there, done that.*

She picked up the new acquisition. The title on the book, and then the author's name, glared up at her... "What the hell?"

The Spring Promise, by CJ Walker.

Kate snapped. She tossed the manuscript sky-high, watching as pages fluttered down around her, clenching her fists. She couldn't believe Jake Willis had a cruel streak, but she'd been wrong. There was nothing for it. Kate put her head down on folded arms and wept.

Chapter 15

"I guess you hated the second book of my series."

The deep voice seeped into her eardrums. Kate sniffled, not looking up, afraid to show her red eyes and stuffed-up nose. She knew the voice, but bit her tongue instead, deciding to play dead.

"You're angry."

Nothing. *You'll have to beg.*

"Furious?"

She snuffled but didn't look up. "You need to keep going through the alphabet, cowboy."

"Pissed off."

"Royally."

"Well, did you at least miss me?"

Kate threw the only weapon she had, a mechanical pencil. It bounced off his coat like a marshmallow. She was too chicken to look him in the eye. "Jerk."

"I am."

"Admissions against interest, you want a prize or something?"

"I want you."

"I told the last guy in here that ship had sailed."

"Who was here?"

"Well, that's so not your business."

"I think it is, Katie."

She shoved back from the desk and dared eye contact—a decision that turned out to be way stupid. He wore a light blue V-neck sweater over a crisp white Oxford shirt, with a printed tie. She wasn't close enough to see the pattern on the neckwear, but the knot was perfect. *Asshole.* Even in the dim light of her desk lamp, Kate was struck by his eyes, which she'd intended to ignore.

He didn't flinch.

At least he wasn't a total clothes horse. The long wool jacket was the same he'd worn on Sunday. The thought of that visit hurt, so she struck out. "How could you?"

He had the decency to look guilty. "How could I what, Katie?"

"Stop it. Stop calling me Katie. I officially revoke my earlier permission for you to do so." She stood and pushed the chair back with enough force it hit the bookcase behind her. Kate wished she had a baseball bat, well, at least a whiffle bat. It would feel great to beat him about the face and neck even if it was only a foam weapon.

"I can explain if you'll let me."

"What? Explain how you seduced me to make sure I read your stupid book?"

"That's not what happened, and you'd already finished it. The book."

"Right."

"I had to go back to Texas."

"Sick cow?"

He didn't comment, instead shuffled back and forth on his feet, his hands in his pockets. Cal didn't break their gaze.

"Sick something."

"I'm sorry. Is someone you love ill? I should act like I care." She was embarrassed about being a complete bitch, even though she was entitled to be outraged. *Went back to Texas, my ass.* There had to be another woman, which meant he'd used her, said those things, and done things that removed all of her inhibition. Years of tamping down emotions, holding back both in love and her scant experience in making love. A lifetime of trying not to turn out like her mother.

"You could say that."

"Well, as I said, I'm sorry. But there's no point in this conversation. You should leave."

"We had a bargain."

"No, you wrote a book with the word 'bargain' in the title and used it against me."

Cal took a few steps toward her, the desk still acting as a moat to keep her safe. Kate knew she'd drop her guard if he even brushed against her arm. He stepped around the desk. "Please don't, Cal."

"I have to."

"It's impossible anyway, don't you see? You write good books, but way too erotic for me, and you live in Texas. You don't have to be here. I bet we have someone who rides horses somewhere on our employee roster, so let's go back to you being a writer and me being an editor who doesn't want to read your stuff. I'll talk to Jake." The entire time Kate had babbled away, Cal was inching along one side of the desk, getting closer.

"Dammit, dammit, dammit, Cal. This won't work."

"It will if you let go of your past, Katie."

"What?"

"You're not your mom, and even if you were, you still deserve love, affection, a family."

"Don't write my life to fix yours."

"Is that what you think I'm doing?"

He was only a foot or so away from her now. Unless she was willing to leap over her desk and dash for the hallway, he'd close the gap. She couldn't stop him unless she ran.

***

Cal's right hand reached up and pushed a strand of hair that had come loose when she tried to demolish his second manuscript. He'd meant to tell her it was a series and he'd finished the second book, but well, they'd gotten sidetracked more than once Sunday evening. He'd left her tucked in bed. She'd been exhausted, and to be honest, so was he. But Will's message had been simple and direct. Cal's prize mare was in breech, and though Will had called the vet, he wanted authority to act if drastic measures were needed.

It seemed easy enough, and he'd kissed Kate while she slept, letting himself out, making sure the lock was in place, although he couldn't slide the deadbolts closed. He was in a cab and on a plane by seven forty. She'd be angry, probably hurt, but Cal realized there was something else he needed from the ranch. Cal had thought to make the trip in two days, but there were complications.

Studying her expression now, he knew it'd be hard to convince Kate he loved her when he'd disappeared for days, and at least in part, over a horse. In hindsight, his behavior was unforgivable. It would be to Kate in any event.

Which was why he shouldn't have been surprised when Kate spun away from him, pulled her purse from a drawer, then slapped him across the face. She left, the door to her office slamming so hard, a woman Cal hadn't yet met came running in. With her cell phone poised in one hand, he imagined she assumed a call to 9-1-1 was in order.

"You okay?"

Cal was rubbing one side of his face, more out of amazement than pain. "I'm fine. I guess I upset the little lady."

"Oh."

He raised an eyebrow in a silent question.

"I see." She looked about the office, manuscript pages strewn everywhere. "I guess that means you're our newest writer. The cowboy, right?"

"Yes, ma'am."

"Please tell me you didn't call Kate 'ma'am'?"

"Guilty."

"Well, then you're lucky she didn't borrow one of those guns you Texans carry around everywhere and shoot you on the spot."

"I reckon she had a right to." His compulsion to be a smart-ass would kill him one day. Since he'd blown it with Kate, it might as well be now rather than later. And why not emphasize his Texas twang, it appeared he'd be going back there for good anyway.

"I'm Marcie from accounting."

"Hello, Accounting Marcie."

"You have a way about you, cowboy, but can I tell you something?"

Cal shrugged his shoulders. She was going to speak her mind no matter what he said or did.

"So, the thing about Kate O'Malley? She always seems uptight, fastidious, careful, quiet, but you know, without making a big deal about it, she's one of the nicest people I've ever met. Which could mean she's not cut out of publishing world cloth, but she loves the work, she's good at it, and despite some folks around here who are stupid and can be mean, Kate is respected and well-liked."

"Some people?"

"Oh, a few girls in production, fact-checking, and her immediate boss, Matt Andrews."

"What did the girls do to upset Kate?"

"Can I be frank?" Cal had a feeling nothing he might say would stop Accounting Marcie from doing that. "They whisper behind her back, but sometimes in a way that Kate either hears it or gets wind of it—ignorami."

"Ignorami?"

"Plural of ignoramus."

"I don't think that's a word."

"You're a writer, aren't you supposed to be creative? I read the manuscript and despite the hot sex, you have a talent for character development, even a little prose."

"You read *The Christmas Bargain?*"

"Of course. Most of us have."

"Do you do that with all the writers?"

"Nope."

"Well, then why my manuscript?"

"I'm trying hard not to put you in the same category as ignorami, Mr. Walker, but it's as if you're a mule, taking to the edge of path so you can see. It's one sure way to fall right off the damned ledge, surefooted or not."

Cal laughed. "I'm not intentionally obtuse."

"Let me help you out then. First of all, the book was brought in by Liz Willis. That brings us all to attention. Then word got out that Kate wouldn't have anything to do with it, and Mr. Willis pressured her into managing the property."

Cal felt like he wasn't physically in the room, but rather sitting in an antiseptic-smelling hospital lobby awaiting the outcome of a difficult procedure being performed on someone he cared about.

"And that's where the intrigue comes in."

"I didn't write a spy novel or a mystery."

"Duh. Liz took your book from the reject stack in the library and insisted next day Jake Willis himself assign it to Kate. She's an editor known to kibosh a bodice ripper with heavy petting, so it meant it was good, but we all know what the ulterior motive was. It's Christmas. That means Liz Willis was gearing up to work her magic."

"My book was in the reject stack?" That was news to Cal, but he brushed off the black and blue marks to his ego. "And what about magic?"

"Oh, Mrs. Willis's matchmaking at Christmas time is officially the stuff of legend."

"And I'm..."

Accounting Marcie folded her arms across the Rudolph applique on her red sweater. Besides the office staff's apparent love for ugly holiday sweaters, she was an attractive woman. Maybe fifty, trim, skirt to the right length for her demeanor and stature, her hair was short but framed her face well. "You see, once Liz gets involved in a book, we folks can't help but take an interest."

"And?"

"Okay, to be honest, I knew who you were when Kate stormed out of here. We googled you. Not to state the obvious or anything, but it seems like you need a primer on this whole love thing." Marcie held up her left hand, palm toward him, fingers stretched upward. "One," pulling her index finger with her right hand so that it folded into her palm, "you're gorgeous, and don't go all blushy on me, you have to know you're good-looking."

Blushy? Cal bit his lip to keep quiet.

"Two," another finger down, "you're independently wealthy, which adds interest and sparked jealousy in some of the staff...and don't interrupt me." Cal had opened his mouth to do that, and with her caution, zipped another comment. She took a deep breath, looking him straight on. "Three, you're a cowboy with significant real estate holdings, you're on several boards in one capacity or another, and you made a large profit with Apple stock. Nice watch." She tapped her wrist with an index finger and nodded at his left arm.

Cal realized he'd been rubbing his jaw off and on during the entire discourse with Marcie. "Thanks." Might as well get all the information he could from Marcie. "Is there a four?"

She dropped her hands to her hips. "Actually, there's more like four through eight, but the bottom line? You were material for office BS, and Kate, well, she's always been given a bad rap about being a prude, stuff like that. And then there was the Santa thing."

"Who knew I'd taken a job as Santa?"

"Pretty much everybody after you pulled your disappearing act this week."

"Four days. And how did y'all find out about it?"

"Matt."

"Kate's supervising editor?"

"And a world-class prick. Sorry, but I've got no nice adjectives for the guy, even if he is in the echelon of senior editors. He's hit on every woman in the office despite warnings and repeat sexual harassment training. We were all kind of hoping he'd be fired. Mr. Willis has given him every chance at modifying his behavior. Anyway, he's still here—"

Cal came around the desk, fast enough to have surprised even himself. "Did he ever hit on Kate?"

"Um…" For the first time in their discussion Marcie ducked her head, evading an answer.

"That's a yes then?"

She looked up and Cal thought the woman might cry. "Oh, he hit on her, he slept with her after she got here two years ago. At least that's the office gossip."

The sick feeling Cal felt well up from his gut was replaced with fury. He pulled out his cell phone, opening the notes app. "Marcie, I want Andrews's address."

"I couldn't."

"You will."

"Promise you won't shoot him?"

"That's ridiculous. Okay, maybe not, but I can't manage being in love with a certain editor unless that asshole is out of the picture."

"You know, cowboy, you might be the best darned tootinest thing that ever happened to this office." Marcie's grin shifted into a chuckle. "It's in the accounting files, and if you ever tell anyone how you got the information…" She was already halfway down the hall, leaving Cal no choice but to run after his new best friend at Bennett & Willis.

***

When the door of the apartment opened, Cal wasted no time. He went at Matt Andrews like a process server. "Are you Matthew Andrews?" Cal fumed at the thought that the man before him— holding what appeared to be a cognac, wearing a pressed linen shirt, and a ridiculous candy cane tie, which was all akimbo— had hurt Kate. No, not just hurt her. This was the asshole who'd slept with Kate.

"Yes, I'm Andrews. You have a package or something for me to sign?"

"Yeah, sign this." Cal's fist connected perfectly with the square jaw on the smug countenance of one smarmy senior editor. Cal leaned over the dazed man, wondering what he'd do if the jerk challenged him further. A football game blared in the background.

"Never," seething, he spoke in a clipped manner, enunciating each word. "Ever. Touch. Speak To. Harass. Or. Even. Look. At. Katie O'Malley. Ever. Again."

He turned and stormed down the stairs, mostly to clear his head and release energy. In all likelihood, had Cal taken the elevator, he would have punched a hole in the veneer siding. When he reached the street, he heard sirens and hoped he hadn't complicated his life further by getting arrested for assault and battery.

Whatever happened, he needed time to think. To resurrect Kate's feelings for him would take work. He loved her, there was no longer any doubt in his mind. In truth, there hadn't been when he left for Texas. One of the reasons was in his coat pocket—his great-grandmother's engagement ring. Somehow, despite all that had happened when his parents died, he'd ended up with the filigreed box. Nobody had ever figured out why Cal refused to give up the can of tennis balls found in his mother's closet. Two well-served balls on the top were all one perceived upon opening the can, but there was no third in the set. Beneath the balls was a cloth bag filled with family heirlooms.

He'd given most of the stuff to his sister, Jenny, because she was older, and hadn't carried the restlessness that haunted Cal beyond her eighteenth year. She was either smarter or luckier than Cal since he continued to drag baggage into everything he did until the moment he'd spied a bookish girl while playing at being Santa Claus.

Hell, who could beat that?

The one-carat miner's-cut diamond was surrounded by miniature pearls, all set in rose gold. And though he had concerns that the large ring wouldn't fit Kate's thin finger, it didn't matter because that's where the damn thing was going whether she liked it or not.

Chapter 16

Jake was pretending to study some papers on his desk when Matt Andrews knocked lightly at his door. "Come in."

"Jake, hi. You wanted to see me?"

"Yes, sit down, Matt."

If Matt thought something was up, he didn't show it, but then again, the shiner around his left eye might have humbled the man at least until the swelling went down and the purple-bluish color started fading to a dull yellow. "That's quite a souvenir on your face, Matt."

"Yeah, I'm still thinking about filing a complaint. It was that damned cowboy, the one who wrote the book you gave O'Malley to manage. So, you have a new assignment for me, Jake?"

Okay, so much for one of Jake's senior editors expressing any humility—ever. "No, in fact, there won't be any further assignments for you, Matt."

"I'm sorry?"

"No, I'm sorry. It's a shame too, because you're good at what you do, editing anyway."

"I'm confused."

"I guess that's fair. I'm not being straightforward, and that's not my style." Jake pulled on an envelope sticking out from under his desk blotter and slid it across his desk to Matt. "Two months' severance pay, your Christmas bonus, which as you know is based on sales, a recommendation as to your editing only, without mention of your abhorrent behavior." Jake looked across at his dumbstruck soon-to-be ex-employee. "I can't disclose much if anyone calls who might hire you, but I can and will say I wouldn't hire you back. In truth? Firing you isn't enough."

"What the fuck?"

"Knock it off, Matt. I should report you to the police, but I've left any complaints that might be out there to your victims."

"My victims?"

"You harass and demean women, Matt. It's probably worse than that, which opens this company up to huge liability, not to mention the cost of defending any EEOC, Civil Rights Act, or Fair Employment and Housing claims. For the sake of all that's holy, Matt, you've put us at a huge risk of exposure. And what matters more? It makes me sick what you may have done to people on our staff." Jake paused, surprised at his fury. "People I care about, Matt."

"You can't do this, Willis."

Noticing the change in address and the likely animosity spilling out of his soon-to-be ex-employee, Jake responded, "I can, and I have, with the approval of all senior partners, as well as Legal. HR documentation supports termination in light of our prior steps, training, re-training, warnings, etc. And despite all that, we may still be open to liability, including some misguided cause of action brought by you against the company. It doesn't matter. You can't stay. Bob Bennett and I held a meeting with staff earlier today. It's been explained to everyone that there will be no ramifications if they choose to come forward now. We've offered counseling if anyone wants or needs it."

"That's bullshit."

"No, Matt. It's not. It's the law, more than necessary, but I'm not losing my life's work to the likes of you or your actions. As to your keys, you can clean out your office this weekend. We went to print on several releases last Monday, so a few key staff members, Bob and I included, will be working this weekend anyway. Hopefully, that will help you with a smooth transition."

"Smooth fucking transition, my ass. I haven't done anything wrong."

"That's the problem, Matt. You don't get it, that your behavior toward office staff, hell, women period, went out with shoe-size cell phones."

Matt stood and yanked the envelope out of Jake's hand. "You haven't heard the last of this, Willis."

"No, Matt, I imagine we haven't, but at least I have the satisfaction of knowing you've no originality of thought. 'Not hearing the last of this' seems a bit dark and stormy nightish, don't you agree?"

"Fuck you." Matt turned and yanked open the door so hard it slammed against the wall. Jake thought he'd be replacing the window glass, but it held. Still, he could hear Andrews cussing and screaming all the way down the hall.

***

The amber liquid held less bite because Jake had let the ice melt while hypnotized by the train chugging around the tree. He smelled Liz before she started rubbing his shoulders from behind the sofa, and then bent to kiss his forehead. He grabbed a wrist and tugged her around the arm of the comfortable couch, pulling her down next to him.

"Kids tucked in?"

"Well, as long as it lasts, yes. They're a little miffed you didn't pop in to say good night, but I know you'll go check on them as soon as you simmer down a bit."

"I'm glad you get me, Lizzie."

"Haven't I always?"

He turned to study his wife's face. Her eyes always sparkled with a hint of "I've got your goat, Jake Willis," and her cheeks were still splattered with freckles as if she'd walked under scaffolding where men were painting. Her fingers rubbing the palm of his hand still had the power of arousal. "You have, Ms. Callahan. You have indeed."

"I'm sorry about Matt Andrews, Jake."

"Yeah? Me too. He's a damned good editor, but what an asshole."

Liz burst out laughing. "Geeze, Jake, that will make a great quote for the newspapers when he sues your ass."

"You know, Mrs. Willis, suing me is suing us."

"Oh sure, I get that. But if we're out on the streets, I'll settle back into writing. A bestseller should help make the mortgage on a falling-down shack somewhere. You know, Caleb Walker has a big Texas spread, bet he'd take us in. You could break horses, the children could learn to round up scorpions, rattlers, and such, and I'd sit in a crowded little room writing the next Dr. Zhivago only with a happily ever after."

"So, you won't be my Lara?"

"God no, Jake. How morbid. Senseless tragedy doesn't become you."

"It did once."

"I'm sorry, sweetheart. I didn't mean to be insensitive about Sam." Liz saddled his lap, taking his drink and setting it aside. "Eighteen years, Jake."

"Long time."

"Not long enough, it will never be long enough. Nine-eleven is a part of all of us who live in New York, hell, a part of all of us in this country. But I'm not jealous, and your first wife will forever have a piece of your heart."

He kissed Liz, figuring the Sam up in heaven would approve. Hopefully, her namesake was sound asleep down the hall because Jake very much needed to express how he felt about Lizzie Callahan in more than words. It had been a brutal day, and he could think of nothing better to cure his ills than making love to his wife.

Lizzie tugged his tie loose and began unbuttoning his work shirt. "You know I think you should get into Uggs and flannel pajama bottoms when you get home at night, right?"

"So not me, Liz."

"So not you."

"Besides, if I went to all that trouble when I first got home, I'd lose the opportunity to watch you starting to take things off me. Your eyes go all smoky, you know."

She kissed him, not a long-married-couple's kiss either. He adored his hot, wicked, lascivious Lizzie. No wonder she found erotica a must-read. "You read another CJ Walker book while I was at the office?"

"Nope."

"Liar."

"I'd already read the second in the series."

"So, you're purring because…"

"I started writing again."

"No kidding?" Jake tugged her closer against him, wanting her to feel his erection. "HEA?"

"It will be, but I decided to try my hand at something a little racier than my usual." This was more whispered in his ear than spoken aloud, and Jake nearly exploded on the spot.

"I have an idea, Mrs. Willis." He blew in her ear, and then tugged gently on her hair so he could see her. "Why don't you read that excerpt to me…" Jake lifted her to his right, stood and pulled her up from the sofa, "in bed."

"Beat ya there." She was gone, running down the hall.

"Damn it. Lizzie. I'm getting too old for this."

But he wasn't.

***

Jake studied the top of his wife's head as she rested on his chest, her fingers tap, tap, tapping on his abdomen. It was a habit from the first time they'd been together, and to his luck, it had happened twice this week alone. That she could still take him to the point of indescribable ecstasy amazed him. That she loved him? He'd still never figure it out, but whatever else she did, Lizzie Callahan had saved him from the darkest place a mind could ever go.

"You're not supposed to be worry-thinking at this moment, Jake."

"I keep wondering when you get older, Lizzie, if you'll lose the ability to read my mind."

"Not going to happen, JW."

"Then what am I thinking right now?"

"Well, I think you were remembering how we got together. It's a different heartbeat when you go back to your past, but then you switched gears."

"I did?"

"Yes, you did." She raised her head and stared at him, squinting in the LED candlelight. "You're now worried about a certain heartbroken editor and our newest writer, Mr. CJ Walker."

"Bingo."

Liz placed a light kiss on his lips, then returned to snuggle mode. "You don't have to fret about that relationship, Jake."

"I don't?"

"Nope."

"Why's that, Liz?"

"Oh Jake. Don't be silly, they're in love. It's going to fix itself."

He wanted to push his wife further on the subject but heard the light snore he loved instead. "Get some sleep, Mrs. Willis." She moaned a bit when he extricated himself and pulled sheets and blankets back around her shoulders.

There were clothes everywhere, but he knew at least that his drawstring pajama bottoms were on a hook in the bathroom. After splashing cold water on his face and gargling mouthwash, Jake flicked the bathroom light off, eased out the master bedroom door, and snuck down the hall to kiss his children good night.

One thing they'd agreed upon after she'd read from her new book: Liz Callahan Willis would have to use a pen name if she intended to pursue writing combustible pages like those that now lay crumpled beneath the sheets. Either way, one thing stayed the same.

If anyone could prophesy what would happen between two heartbroken lovers, it was Liz.

Chapter 17

"There's nothing like a Santa-Cowboy to sweep a girl off her feet, Cal," Saul teased.

Cal grinned back at the corner market proprietor. The man was a major help. Of course, Cal thought ruefully, it didn't hurt that the man thought of Kate as one of his own. The loading dock was a fine place for a horse trailer, and though Cal would have preferred to be riding one of his animals, the stables at Central Park had been more than accommodating once Cal put enough money down that the payment covered the purchase price of two horses.

"You know, Saul, I hardly know you, and yet somehow it seems like you've been a friend all my life."

"Well, I got roots, son."

"How so?"

"A great-uncle who headed west after the Civil War. Wound up running a small newspaper in the Arizona Territory."

"Not quite Texas."

"Maybe not, but I got a bunch of family in what was once the wild west. A card comes every year, a long-standing joke I guess. They do a sepia photo of everybody even remotely related to Uncle Jacob. Pretty funny seeing a nice Jewish family in Western garb, six-shooters, gun belts, and standing at the entrance to his one-time newspaper office. It's a high-end brewery now, go figure."

"Yeah, I guess family can surprise you, but it's nice that you can trace your roots back that far. You're welcome at the ranch anytime, Saul. By the way, if I didn't say it already, Happy Hanukkah."

"Sure, sure. You know, Cal, family is in the heart. You can have your own without necessarily having a past. I think you might have it with our Kate. If I wasn't damned sure about it, there's no way you'd be parking a horse trailer in my loading area on Christmas Eve."

"Luck or fate, Saul?"

"It's too weird to be luck, son. It's more like the hand of God the way I see it."

"I guess I believe in something, Saul."

"Doesn't have to be much, CJ. Try believing in that girl, and God will take care of the rest."

Cal turned away from his new friend. The stable had assured him the young man who'd stay with the trailer was reliable. Cal had a generator that kept the rental warm, with fresh hay, a small latrine, and a mini-fridge. That should handle everything for the two hours Cal needed to convince Kate they belonged together. And he only planned to use the horse if Kate proved to be as stubborn as last Thursday in the office. He rubbed his jaw in memory.

Cal might be a damned good cowboy, but he wasn't betting on his skills as a white knight.

***

Christmas Eve. Kate watched the little HO train go around and around her tree. She'd gone hog-wild decorating the thing. The festivities included a Louis Roderer cork with the wire basket thingy that once held it in the bottle, an old comb from her bathroom drawer, a handful of gold and red glass balls, super cheap from one of those dollar stores, and a small article from the last page of the business news. "Bennett & Willis fires senior editor." Few details, but she thought the news piece added something, if nothing else, closure to another chapter of her life.

"*Adios*, Matt."

She toasted the tree with a club soda and smiled at her string of hardened breadsticks. It resembled a mobile, representing the likelihood a part of her life that had barely gotten off the starting line was over.

Caleb Jethro Walker.

Hell, it wouldn't have lasted anyway. The idea that she could have an HEA with a cowboy whose middle name was Jethro was too far-fetched.

You couldn't write that shi…stuff. But it hurt. At least the breadsticks stood for a good night in her life. No, a milestone. A part of herself was buried because of childhood scars, the lifelong specter that she would be like her mother.

Two amazing Caleb Walker episodes. That's what Kate labeled them now. So what if the ramifications came back to haunt her, or that her heart was in pieces. At least now she knew she could enjoy sex. Except that the man may have ruined her for any other relationships, for-freaking-ever. Her brain felt like a yo-yo, going back and forth with the what-ifs and what-have-I- dones.

And Kate hadn't melted into a loose woman with anyone. It had been possible because she was falling in love.

"Bah humbug."

Tears slipped over her cheek. She tried swatting the moisture away. Anyway, who cared? Caleb the cowboy, aka hot department-store-cad-Santa, wouldn't be in town much longer. He'd probably already left for that damned horse ranch after the last-minute Santa visits. The department store had closed early for Christmas Eve. Liz had let it slip that he was there working.

Okay, Liz Callahan never let anything slip, but Kate had ignored the bait.

The most she expected of Cal now was to wake up and find some lumps of coal in the pitiful stocking she'd laid over the back of a sofa cushion. Kate swiped at more tears. "Dammit, knock it off, Kate." Flopping back on the couch allowed her to stop staring at the stupid CJ Walker train and study her slippers instead. Blue Smurfs—cute, stupid, and immature. All the parts of her personality that served as protection against accepting her destiny.

Behind closed eyelids, Kate saw the headline of herself five years down the road. "Lonely Editor Leaving Cat Shelter Killed When Struck By City Bus." She didn't even like cats, and the vision was so ridiculous she laughed aloud. She opened her eyes, studying herself from outstretched legs down. She loved the blue flannel pajama bottoms. There were penguins stamped like a South Pole parade on the fabric. That she celebrated the opposing pole in her choice of attire should piss Santa off.

Cal in his Santa outfit flashed across her brain like a neon sign on Broadway. It didn't matter what the big jerk wore, he was gorgeous. All that fake beard and stuff and his sparkling eyes. like in his book. Except Santa didn't screw a gullible editor and leave her brokenhearted.

Kate sat bolt upright. *I should get drunk*. Sure, the recent forays into alcohol could be a reason for her current predicament, but she didn't need an excuse because it was Christmas Eve. And if she got stupid, she'd wake up Christmas day with a hangover and a big puffy face. If she felt bad enough, she could make an excuse to skip the invitation to visit the Willises for a regular old Christmas dinner. She smacked the throw pillow and clutched it to her stomach with a clenched fist. Whether it was out of frustration, anger, or because her heart ached, she didn't care.

Kate *wanted* to go to Liz and Jake's. She wanted to be a part of Christmas with someone, anyone. She didn't blame Liz for trying to set her up with Cal. Besides, the situation was, in part, her fault. She could have said no.

"Hey, it's Christmas Eve, how about music?" The empty apartment seemed to agree with the idea, so Kate jumped off the couch and cranked up the stereo. She'd already pre-set her favorite holiday station. It was one that mixed Christmas movie songs, carols including classical and modern, rock and roll, even some '90s grunge bands. She wasn't disappointed.

"You're a mean one, Mister Grinch." Kate sang along all the way to the refrigerator, Pulling out her trusty Chardonnay, she poured. "Kind of like a trusty six-shooter." Ha. Ha. Funny. She rejoined the song, "You are a heel…" and slugged the glass of wine. Putting the crystal down on the bar, she added, "Set 'em up, barkeep." She could be a cowboy too. Acting both parts, she played the role of a bartender and filled the glass to the brim, drinking another two-thirds of it, then went back to her song, dancing around the living room, doing a little soft-Smurf-slipper-shuffle.

"You're as cuddly as a cactus…" The buzzer sounded from down below, and since she was expecting pizza, she hit the response button. Thirty dollars in various forms of change sat in a bowl next to the front door. She thought the delivery and pizza totaled about that much, but what about a tip? Well, it was Christmas Eve, so she pulled an extra ten out of her wallet. "You're as charming as an…" She always ordered pizza from the same place and knew all three of the delivery people well enough that she opened the door when the bell rang. "an… Santa?"

He was too good-looking, too tall, and so not the pizza delivery kid, as he sported the department store hat and fake beard. "You're not my pizza." Kate turned away, ignoring CJ Walker, the very next best thing in hot, next to a pie. "I bet you have garlic in your soul, Mister Santa."

Kate spun away, and between the soft fabric soles of her slippers and the waxed floor, she almost fell on her ass. Except her ass was once again in the arms of the no-good Nick, Cal Walker. "Grinch."

"Katie."

"Ms. O'Malley to you, buster."

"You're drunk."

"Trying to be."

"Okay." Cal carried Kate to the couch, set her down, and took the wineglass out of her hand. "And you've been crying."

"Ya think? Mister Grinch is a bad banana, but you...you, you're badass."

Cal hadn't kicked the door closed when he'd kidnapped her from the foyer to the sofa, and over his shoulder, Kate saw one of her three usual "Slice-oh-Heaven-Pizza & Pasta To Go" guys.

"Ms. O'Malley?"

She tried to get up off the couch. "Pizza man..."

***

Not that it took much effort, but Cal gently pushed Kate back onto the sofa. "Hold still. I'll get the pizza."

"You okay, Ms. O'Malley?" the pizza man asked. Cal, frustrated, moved to pay for the pie and included a one-hundred-dollar bill as an incentive for the gopher to leave.

"I'm as fond of a giant tip as the next guy, sir, but I'm not leaving until Ms. O'Malley tells me it's okay."

"Hey, Derrick. Is the pie hot?"

"Yes."

"Extra cheese and double sausage?"

"As always."

"Did Santa give you a tip?"

"Too much of one, Ms. O'Malley."

"Well, he's like that. He's a cowboy, you know. I'm okay, Derrick. But you better go now. It's Christmas Eve, you must have other pizzas to deliver, and it's okay. I know Mr. Claus. He won't shoot me."

"Okay."

Cal studied the young man, catching suspicion in his expression as he surveyed Kate's situation. The pizza kid returned his focus to Cal, who stood like a bodyguard, still holding out money for the cost of the food in one hand, the large bill for a tip in the other.

"Here's my card, son. Ms. O'Malley is my editor for a new book."

"You write romance?"

"Yeah, and who'd make up a story like that, right?"

The young man looked over Cal's left shoulder. Cal got it. He understood pizza deliveries would probably be made by the same person, or maybe one or two different kids, and that Kate might order a lot of pizza. She got home late most nights, so could order from the office. The pizza in the kid's warming bag was cooked already though, so Kate obviously had more than one resource for delivered food. A hot pizza would be better as far as timing than the take-and-bake variety he'd picked up on her behalf two weeks ago. Plus, a prepared meal meant she could burn the midnight oil at the office, place the order when she left, and still be home to turn on lights, the TV, and pour a glass of wine.

It dawned on him that given Kate's isolated lifestyle, she'd make friends with the person who buzzed, came up the stairs, knocked, and handed over her dinner. The loneliness she must face pulled at Cal's heart. He loved Kate O'Malley, and he'd convince her of it tonight, or...

"It's okay, Derrick. I don't know Santa, I *know* him. Wink-wink. Santa-cowboy is an intimate friend..." Kate giggled at her remark. "I mean, I've read his book and stuff, of course."

` "Okay, well, if you're sure."

"Merry Christmas. And to your family, say hi from me."

"Merry Christmas, Ms. O'Malley." He turned, and Cal closed and bolted the door.

Putting the large flat box on the bar, he turned and crossed to the blasting stereo, lowering the warbled carols to a bearable volume. When he sat down on the sofa, he had to lift her feet, so that now the eyes of one slipper seemed to be staring him down. "You're unbelievably cute, Ms. O'Malley. Ridiculously cute, indeed." His comment went unanswered, the whistle of a soft snore reaching his ears.

Rather than be cross-examined by a couple of inanimate Smurfs, Cal extricated himself from beneath Kate's calves and busied himself by straightening up the kitchen and setting out plates and some forks. He put the pizza on a cookie tray rummaged from a drawer under the stove and set the extra-cheese, double-sausage, heart-stopping dinner on low in the oven. If the girl ate as much pizza as it appeared, it should be easy to convince her to have steak once in a while. At least she couldn't bitch about cholesterol or fat.

He opened the champagne he'd brought, admitting to himself it had been nice to see Saul again. That the man was willing to let him put the horse trailer in the back for the night was of extra benefit. Cal was still trying to figure out how to pull off the white knight bit if he needed it. Still, it had supplied courage when the shop owner had given Cal the thumbs-up for his planned caper.

Oh, there'd been a bit of a veiled threat about Kate, as in, "You hurt that girl, I have friends, not necessarily of my faith, but live-and-let-live buddies who will find you, maybe rearrange your face a little." But then Saul had slapped Cal on the shoulder. "Who am I kidding. I couldn't hurt you. Kate would kill me for it."

Cal returned to the sofa and again sat with Kate's feet in his lap, enjoying how the green thermal t-shirt clung to her small but beautiful breasts and the way her diaphragm rose and fell with each breath. Her face was a bit puffy, which proved his theory. She'd been crying when he first showed up. He'd expected nothing less than a cross between "royally pissed off," as she'd noted in their last conversation, and embarrassed. That she'd been sad gave him hope.

Cal was determined to avoid another fight. The ring was no longer in his coat pocket. He'd carried the outer wool garment over his arm when he arrived on account of the Santa outfit. His trusty wool duster now hung in the hall closet. *Might as well move in, make it harder for Kate to boot my ass out the door.* She wouldn't be able to see the train lying on the sofa, so he'd have to wake her up, propose, then lead her to the caboose with the ring tucked inside.

Kate stirred, and when she did, Cal tried to figure out how he'd keep her from throwing him out before he could explain.

***

Shit, triple shit. *Sorry,* God. Swearing on Christmas Eve. Geeze. But he was here, she could sense him, and besides, Kate remembered her Mister Grinch solo and the sensation of being lifted and plopped on the sofa. Okay, it hadn't been plopping per se, he'd been gentle. And there'd been an exchange with her usual pizza delivery person. But now her head hurt, she was hungry, she still wanted to get drunk, and more importantly, kick his sorry butt out of her life.

"You don't want me to leave, do you, Katie?"

"Huh?" *I should play dumb.* His voice was so beautiful, his hands rubbed her feet through the worn soles of the Smurfs, and the sensation was soothing. "Wait a minute. I'm totally pissed off at you...you moron."

"You're awake."

"Duh."

"I was surprised to hear you sing. Nice voice, Katie."

"Poop, cowboy. Horse poop at that."

"Okay, I'm not saying you should join a choir, but that was a decent rendition of 'Mister Grinch.'"

"You should know. You're a cross between Simon Legree, Genghis Khan, and the jerk who stole Whoville." He sipped champagne from a glass. *Is he drinking champagne without me? He is a jerk.*

"For an educated woman, you certainly have a gutter mouth."

"I didn't swear."

"You were thinking something nasty about me, your eyes read like a ticker tape. Moron's okay though, let's stick with moron."

"Why?"

"Because that much is true. I'm a moron."

"Nah, you're smart." She held up the flat of her hand as if to repel him, should he make a move in her direction. "Unmitigated ass?"

"I'm not going to argue, Kate."

She was momentarily disappointed that he'd used Kate instead of Katie. "So, why are you here?"

"Simple."

"I don't want to play games."

"Okay. Here goes."

He shuffled a bit, and as if expecting something like a kick to his chin, he continued to hold her ankles above the opening of the blue fuzzy slippers. "Because, Katie O'Malley, I'm in love with you."

"Shit."

"I'm never sure what you mean when you say that. Sometimes it's a good shit, other times not so much."

"You left me."

"I went to Texas."

"Same difference."

"No, it's not."

I will not cry, I will not cry, I will not cry. Tears poured down her face despite the resolve. She wanted to say something but didn't know what. "We made love, you left without saying good-bye, and you went back to Texas."

"I had to go, Katie."

She tugged her feet away, sitting up and crunching her body into the end of the sofa. "Why?"

"A few reasons."

"Name one."

"A famous bloodline was in danger. My best mare was in breech."

Well, that hurt. "You left me for a horse?" She tried her best drawl. "Shit-howdy, don't that beat all." That was arguably Kate's best accent ever, only maybe she'd gone over the top a little too Southern. Well, hell, she'd never been to Texas.

"You're going to like Texas, Katie."

"The hell I am, you buffoon."

"Quite an extensive vocabulary you have, given your editorial position. Anyway, I figure we'll go there maybe twice a year, for a few weeks at a time, spring and fall."

"Oh? Dare I ask why those two seasons?"

"Sure. It's birthing time for the cattle. Baby cows are cute."

"What man says 'cute' anyway?"

He ignored her, which she deserved.

"And autumn in my part of the state is beautiful. "

"You've been on the range too long, cowboy. I ain't goin' nowhere with little old you."

"Not even Paris?"

"Cowboy, you make absolutely no sense. And how can anyone take you seriously when you're sitting there in that Santa suit, beard and all?"

"Because I've arranged to do a charitable thing this evening. It's still early. Folks are out in your neighborhood, people are still working in stores and restaurants."

"Yeah, so?"

"Do you have any warm clothes?"

"That's like such a stupid question, I live in New York, you—"

"Moron?" He smiled. "You've no reason to trust me, but will you, please? It'll make you feel good."

"Hmph." But she gave in, the idea of being outside, the elements, seeing other people besides him, were all reasons besides being with him. She'd give him that much. Only a teeny bit of her. Period.

Chapter 18

Kate stared up at her cowboy. He was sitting on a horse, in full Santa getup, a set of saddlebags draped over the horse's neck, and his hand out. "I'm not getting on that horse with you, Claus."

"'Course you are. You're my elf. I can't do this without you, Katie."

She'd already been introduced to Tim, an employee of a stable who wanted to get home for Christmas Eve but was getting paid too much by Kate's tycoon-writer to turn down the job. "Well, that's handy." She motioned to the stepladder that appeared out of nowhere.

"Ma'am?"

She gave the young helper the stink eye.

"I'm afraid Ms. O'Malley detests the term 'ma'am,' Tim."

Kate would have punched CJ Walker in the nose if he wasn't impossible to reach. "What's this ridiculous plan, Cal?"

"Secret stuff. I'll whisper it in your ear once you're settled up here. With me."

"I am so not getting on behind you on the back of that horse."

"Nope, you're not." Cal slid back in the saddle and patted the area behind the horn. "You'll be here, up front. You can grab the horn if you get scared. One hour, that's all I'm asking. One hour to serve the neighborhood you love."

Damn the cowboy for going all philanthropic on her and tossing a little guilt into the equation. Tim wrapped his arms for warmth, stomping his boots, no doubt to circulate blood into his limbs. It hadn't started snowing again yet, but the temperature had dropped at least five degrees since she'd followed Cal down the steps of her building and the half block to Saul's market. Inhaling for courage, Kate started up the stepladder as Tim reached to hold it steady. The big horse snorted but didn't flinch when she let Cal lift her the rest of the way into the saddle.

"Geeze, how am I supposed to get down?"

"Oh, let's cross that bridge when we come to it, sweetheart."

"So trite, and I am not your sweetheart."

"I'm working on that, Katie." The last had been spoken into her ear, the heat of his breath threatening her stability on the saddle. "Oh, and you need this."

"What?"

He didn't answer her, instead he pulled a green felt hat over her head and ears. "You've been officially sworn in as one of Santa's elves, ma'am, you've got to believe."

"In what?"

"Santa Claus." Cal's other conspirator whisked the stepladder away. "Figure an hour tops, and I'll bring Duke back. You might as well re-hitch the trailer so you don't have to spend all night getting back to the stables. Thanks for the help, Tim, what with it being Christmas Eve and all."

"No problem, Mr. Walker. You're paying, and my girl's a nurse. She's earning triple time tonight. We'll celebrate the holiday in the morning, knowing our little house fund is growing."

Cal turned the horse down the alley, the clop, clop, clop of hooves on cement at odds with the silence that came on the crest of snow. A flake fell on the horse's mane but didn't stick. "You know it's going to snow, right?"

"Horse has a winter coat, he won't mind it for a bit. Besides, I paid for him to have a good rubdown and extra oats."

"Geeze, I'm sure Duke, is that the horse's name, Duke?" Kate shifted in the saddle.

"Yep."

"Well, I'm sure he'll appreciate it, but that poor young man, out like this on Christmas Eve."

"You live here, Katie. You know the hacks will drive tourists around Central Park for another hour or two, at least. Good money on a holiday, a lot of happy people drinking and tipping."

"If you don't mind my asking, how much did you contribute to Tim's house fund?"

"Don't mind at all, Katie. I plan on sharing everything with you, and knowing your penchant for propriety, you will lecture me half the time. Still, so you know, Tim's girl, as he calls her, is his wife, and she's six months pregnant. They've been saving up for a house over there across the river," he pointed in the general direction of the Hudson, "somewhere, I'll learn my way around one of these days. Anyway, I helped out a little."

"What's a little?"

"I have a lot of money, Kate."

"What's a little, Cal?"

"Five grand."

"Are you freaking kidding me?"

"Nope."

"That's nuts. I knew it. You're crazy."

"Little bit." He tugged her elf cap down farther, barely glancing her neck with his gloved hand, yet it still sent shivers from ears to her toes."

"You cold, darlin'?"

"No. And nothing you say will convince me you aren't a completely crazy and irresponsible person. I need to amend that observation to include out of your mind. That said, what the hell are we doing?"

"It wasn't that much for me, and Tim promised they'd name the baby after me."

"Can you answer my question instead of a dodge?"

"If it's a girl, she'll be Jethro Tina."

Her head snapped to look at him, the move forced a turn in the saddle, and she slammed her right thigh on the horn. "Ow. Dammit to hell."

"Hmmm, not the right night to be shouting that aloud. Hope that doesn't bruise." He smiled down at her, It looked like concern, but Kate wasn't sure, although there was enough light from streetlamps and storefronts.

"It's not even legal to do this, ride around Tribeca on horseback."

"Maybe not, but we're only going a few blocks, seeing some places you probably order or pick up wine from, I imagine."

Kate had no comeback, and they rode in silence for a minute or two. It was awkward in the saddle, and she couldn't help but settle into him, her rear end between his muscled thighs, pressing against his groin. Snow started drifting down slowly from above. It was beautiful, and what the hell, she was on a horse, with the man she loved, even if she had no intention of telling him what was in her heart. All of this on Christmas Eve. Nobody could write this story, let alone believe it, but... "Hey, that's Armando's Deli."

"It is. Six staff, and Mando on duty until 11:30 tonight."

"What? Are you a spy or something?"

"No. Stalker, remember? I did a little research is all. Reach in that saddlebag, the one on your left, fish out seven envelopes."

"Why?"

Cal ignored Kate, and leaning into her, both reins in one hand, used his left arm to complete the task she'd ignored. In the process, he brushed against her breast. Recollections of that night together rushed her like an oncoming train. It felt so good, he smelled good, everything about being next to him, even the horse, with snorts in the frigid air showing as steam, his voice resonant, his chest pushing against her back. Kate wanted to melt into her cowboy, except she'd been such a bitch, he might not let it happen.

"Because it's Christmas, Katie."

It didn't take long for Armando to accept the envelopes and hand one each to his staff, tucking the seventh in his butcher's coat pocket. "Thanks, Santa. I don't need this but..." He gestured to his workers, who, having opened their envelopes, were gesticulating and laughing and expressing thanks to Kate's Santa. "It's a good thing you do here. Hard workers, families, you make a little more Christmas, I think."

"Does me more good than you know, Armando. Besides, it's a tax deduction." Cal laughed and turned the horse around the corner. Kate was getting cold and pushed herself further into Cal's form. His fake beard tickled the back of her neck.

For about thirty minutes or so, they rode together, distributing envelopes to the handful of establishments still open, and every owner, chef, clerk, or staff member seemed to know they were coming. Even the police officer on the last corner smiled.

Cal pulled up. "Hello, Sergeant. Merry Christmas."

"Thanks, Cal. You going to have that animal off the street in ten minutes like you promised?"

"Yes, sir. Did the association get my check?"

"Your donation was too generous, but that's not why the captain gave you that special permit for this little jaunt of yours. Apparently you promised to create a character based on him in your next book?"

"Something like that. You want in?"

"No, thanks. Anonymity and plain living's fine for me and the missus." He stepped back from the horse. "It's going to start coming down soon." The officer's cap was proof of that, as a ridge of snow was forming on the brim. "Merry Christmas, and might I add, you make a right fine elf, miss."

The sergeant was a wise man, and Kate guessed he opted for "miss" over "ma'am" nine times out of ten. He'd live longer that way.

Cal wrapped a blanket that materialized out of nowhere around her shoulders, and between the rhythmic walk of the horse, resting against him in a cocoon, she snoozed, waking up only when she felt Cal slip from the saddle.

"Huh?"

"Come on, Katie. Lean down a little."

She didn't object, sliding from the horse into his arms. Next thing she remembered was Saul helping her into his little Fiat. She was curling into the seat when he opened the driver's side door and put a foot on the car's frame. "I'll get her to the apartment, CJ. You square things with Tim and meet us there."

"Got it, and thanks, Saul. That there's precious cargo."

Saul grinned. "And an elf to boot. Happy holidays, son. And good luck."

She might have wondered about the good luck comment, but she was too happy having been appointed as precious cargo to care.

Chapter 19

"How come you get to drink champagne, and I don't?" Kate asked aggrievedly. Cal chuckled and handed Kate his glass, which was still half full. She narrowed her eyes. *It would have to do.*

"Knock yourself out, Madam Editor."

She started to get up, but he was too quick. "Katie O'Malley, you will sit still for one minute and hear me out." She could feel his strength. He wasn't hurting her, but he meant it, so she let out an exasperated sigh and shrugged her shoulders.

"Go on."

"I know now that my ranch foreman can handle about anything. In fact, I've already apologized to him for second-guessing his abilities. I also know," his eyes locked with Kate's, those damnable dimples went into overdrive when he ducked his head with a sheepish grin, "that I love you, and I think I ran. No, I admit I ran. I didn't see it then, but when you wouldn't take my calls after I got back, I had to self-analyze what it is that trips me up in relationships."

"You've had a lot of women?"

"No. But it goes beyond you and me. It's friends, my sister... I spent twenty-plus years of my life in a self-preservation mode."

"You said you were in foster care."

"My parents died in a plane crash."

"Oh, sweet Jesus, I'm sorry, Cal."

"It was a long time ago."

"I'm still sorry." He nodded in appreciation. Then he ran two fingers along her shoulder, down to her hand, and started tracing her fingers. The sensation knocked her inner guards off their pedestals. One by one her objections fell away, like crumbling turrets, the walls she'd built around her fears of rejection, of her sexuality, tumbling, tumbling down.

"So, could we back up a little bit?"

"To what, something I said?"

"Yes."

"What part?"

"Gosh, Caleb, please don't make me beg."

"Oh, but that's the fun part, Ms. O'Malley."

Kate didn't mean to, but a deep moan escaped when he kissed her knuckles, then her wrist, her palm, his fingers released, and his hand reached up to her face. He traced her lips. "What part, Katie?"

"Um, something about love, I think."

"Oh, that?"

"Please, cowboy."

"I love you, Kate."

"Okay, then everything's okay, sort of. In any event, I un-dub thee moron."

He laughed aloud, right before his mouth found hers. The kiss was deep, searching, and Kate didn't resist. She could be Wendy Avalon, not quite a porn star, but a woman in love with a handsome cowboy-Santa.

Their lovemaking was tender and slow as they came together spontaneously, the emotions afterwards overwhelming them both. Kate's Smurf slippers were on two ends of the room, pajama bottoms slung over the sofa. She'd no idea where Cal's clothes were, although his shirt was still on, albeit open to his bare skin. She would need to lecture him about that. If he were a cowboy as he said, then he should have some snap-type shirts, the kinds where the front and the cuffs released with a tug. He had the one from the subway. They'd start with that.

Good thing the sofa was wide because they now lay side by side, mostly naked, the room dark except for the few lights on the tree behind them. "Shit."

"My dear articulate girl. Now what?"

"My pizza."

"It's in the fridge. I put it away when you took that hot shower. Difficult not to join you but I wanted to wait."

"Writer, cowboy, Santa, and now a pizza saver. Yikes. But it might be dead, the pizza, it got here hours ago. It was here before you did that thing…"

"What thing was that, Ms. O'Malley?"

"That horse thing, the gifts, and snow, and the..." She paused, not sure she should say any more.

"For an editor, you have the clarity of a dark night."

"That's dark and stormy night to you, cowboy."

"You were saying?"

"You know we don't have the same political beliefs, right?"

"Kate, fat babies fart, and their mothers still love them."

"Okay. Was that a non sequitur? Because I think it was."

"You want to keep making objections, or admit you like me?"

"I was going to say that I couldn't do this...at least before you rode into my life like some white knight."

"Ah, that. You don't truly care about the pizza, do you, Katie?"

"You wouldn't say that if you were hungry enough to eat a horse. Oops, sorry."

Cal flicked a nipple with his index finger. "Ow."

"Horses are nice, Kate."

"I know, but I'm never getting on one again."

"We'll see. You might learn to love it. Rubbing back and forth in a saddle..." Her fist connected with his upper arm.

"Hey."

She pulled away, nearly tripping over his Santa Claus coat. Finding her tee on the floor, she tugged it over her head. In two minutes, she dressed, and when she came out of the bathroom, Cal had set pizza slices on plates on the table, along with two glasses of champagne, forks and paper towels for napkins. He'd turned the lamp on at the far end of the easy chair, and the little train still chug-chugged around the tiny tree.

"Microwaved. It won't kill you, so sit."

"That a command or a request, cowboy?"

"A request."

"Did the department store fire you when you left town?"

"No, I called, but I finished my contract. I had to work this afternoon, in fact. Busy Santa, a lot of big wishes from children and harried parents, it being Christmas Eve and all."

Kate stared at him, "You were here? Never mind. I knew that."

"Well then, you can't be upset that I kept playing Santa after trying to earn your forgiveness last Friday."

"Dammit, Cal."

"Please tell me you're not going back into royally pissed off mode."

"Well, I was furious, I knew you were in town. So, the righteously indignant thing was kind of a tease. Liz let it slip."

They said it at the same time: "Liz Callahan doesn't let anything slip."

With laughter, they settled into companionable silence, taking a few bites of pizza each. "Can you cook, cowboy? Besides, pizza, I mean."

"Steak."

She laughed aloud. "Yeah, I guess steak will keep me satisfied."

"I'll keep you satisfied, Katie." And that officially made her blush. The sensation that arose from under her skin and tracked her nerve endings like a satellite signal whenever he looked at her returned.

She'd have to give up the ruse. Kate was in love. No point in holding on to her armor. Caleb Walker was the "just right" chair, the "just right" porridge, and the heavens knew he was "just right" in bed. Her Santa-Cowboy was also funny, kind, and GQ handsome.

Pushing his chair back, Cal stood, reached across the table and stopped the little train.

"Hey, what gives."

"Present on the train."

"You got me a present? Oh Cal, I don't have anything for you."

"Yeah, you do." She wondered at his expression, and the comment warranted his usual sly grin, but he looked almost frightened. "It's in the caboose."

"What is?"

"The present."

Kate licked her fingers, then sipped at her champagne, enjoying the small tic in his right cheek. Caleb Jethro Walker was nervous. At least, it seemed that way. Time would reveal their tells, no doubt, and she didn't need to torture him, so she reached out, and the fingers of her right hand touched inside the small opening to the train car. "What..." The object was round and cool to the touch. She slipped it over the top of her right index finger, gently extricating the item. "Cal?"

"It was my great-grandmother's. I don't have much family left, but you'll like my sister and her kids. I mean, I hope you will."

"Cal, I—"

"You said you don't have a present for me, Kate."

"I don't."

"You do." He reached over and gently slid the ring on her left ring finger.

"I'm confused."

"Say yes, Katie. That's all I want for Christmas. Say yes."

She looked down at her hand, back up to Cal's face, to the ring again, and then into his eyes., with a look that said it all, including his desire for her and hopes for them. She pushed back her chair and took the few steps toward him.

"Katie?"

"I got something to say, cowboy, but it ain't yes." She couldn't stand the stricken look a second longer. "How about yee-haw?" Kate pressed her hands against his shoulders, and turning him, pushed gently so that he sat back down in the chair. Then, she straddled his legs and settled on to his thighs, kissing his nose, his eyes, his lips, and that's how Cal got his answer.

The chair tipped backwards and they were on the floor. "Yee-haw, cowboy. Shit howdy, yes. The answer's yes. I guess now I get to call you Jethro."

His smile wiped nearly every bad memory and pain in her life away, and though she knew there'd be moments when her past forced all that insecurity back to the surface, Kate was safe now. The clock tower in the bank building down the street started chiming, and people below her window were shouting Merry Christmas.

"It's midnight, Katie."

"So it is. Merry Christmas, Jethro."

"Merry Christmas back, Wendy Avalon."

"Touché, Claus. Now is it okay with you if we celebrate Christmas in bed instead of on the floor?"

He laughed as he kissed her again. "Not a snowball's chance in hell, ma'am."

Leave it to a writer to ring in the holiday with a too-trite phrase.

Oh well. It turned out, Kate had a lifetime to edit that kind of crap.

ABOUT THE AUTHOR

Joan traces her roots back to Ireland, England, and Wales. Discounting any inherited pioneer courage, she recently left her home of forty-plus years, and her state of four generations, for the mountains of northern Arizona. Instead of musing the fates of a hero or heroine along a foggy beach, she now hikes trails looking out to Granite Mountain or the San Francisco Peaks. Petrified, sure, but she loves her small-town peppered with rodeos, lakes, pines, old trucks, and rocks - lots of rocks. The transition made by moving truck instead of covered wagon allowed her to settle into writing full-time and lawyering part-time. While support from her four sisters, her children, their spouses, and a crew of grandchildren is a constant, her cowboy-hero husband remains her best bud along with her Labradoodle, Doobie, who practices goofiness, toy-mongering, and provides constructive criticism of character arcs in exchange for walks.

JOAN WOULD LOVE TO HEAR FROM YOU:

FB: facebook.com/joan.m.bird

twitter: @AuthorJoanMBird

www.BOROUGHSPUBLISHINGGROUP.com

If you enjoyed this book, please write a review. Our authors appreciate the feedback, and it helps future readers find books they love. We welcome your comments and invite you to send them to info@boroughspublishinggroup.com. Follow us on Facebook, Twitter and Instagram, and be sure to sign up for our newsletter for surprises and new releases from your favorite authors.

Are you an aspiring writer? Check out www.boroughspublishinggroup.com/submit and see if we can help you make your dreams come true.

www.ingramcontent.com/pod-product-compliance
Lightning Source LLC
Chambersburg PA
CBHW051253170626
46809CB00004B/1622